A CIP catalogue record for this book is available from the British Library.

ISBN 978-1-980-58442-1

Cover images © Canva (www.canva.com)

Chapter 1

100% Battery Left

It was the school holidays and Fiona Chen was looking forward to a week away from maths, bullies and getting up at seven in the morning. Her parents were taking her and her sister Molly on their annual camping trip to the Lake District. Fiona's father Simon was complaining because apparently the weather man had given out a severe weather warning for Cumbria and there was lots of wind and rain coming. Fiona begin to think about the weather man and how powerful he must be. *How can one man control all the world's weather?*

Fiona's mother Julie was telling her father not to be such a stick in the mud. Fiona guessed that this must mean it was going to be both muddy and sticky where they were camping, so Fiona was not entirely thrilled by the idea of going either. But it was still better than maths, bullies and being dragged out of bed and away from her dreams. Away from her dreams, and her smartphone.

Although Fiona was sleepy that morning, their semi-detached townhouse on Sycamore Drive was awake with activity. Stationed in her bedroom, she listened to the mechanics of the house play out to her like a faithful orchestra. Firstly, the washing machine door clicking shut, the whirring to life of its motor as it began to release water, the clinking of a cardigan zip beating against the metal drum as it began its spin cycle. Then came the bleeping sound of an iron heated up and ready for use on Simon's shirts. The clattering of pans in the kitchen cupboard was next, as the kitchen was slowly tidied up. After that, the squawking of the water pump in the upper bathroom as the en-suite shower came to life. Fiona thought that the house sounded more like a factory than a home.

The paper thin walls of the newly-built house meant that Fiona could even hear everyone's conversations. She heard her mother down in the kitchen say to Molly, 'Go and check on your sister, make sure she has packed her things, okay dear?' She spoke with a slight Chinese accent because she wasn't born in England.

Fiona heard Molly reply in her British accent, 'She hasn't even started yet. She's just playing with her phone, like always.' One of the bullies in school had referred to her as BBC. For a long time this convinced Fiona that she belonged to a television company. Then she discovered that BBC stood for British Born Chinese.

Sat cross-legged on the floor, Fiona screwed up her face in annoyance. *My little sister is always dobbing me in!* Fiona glanced across her bedroom, taking in the sights of her lair. For a while she stared at her own face in the mirror, wondering who she was supposed to be. She was half-Chinese, half British. Her eyes were blue and her cheeks were full. Her skin was the colour of a late autumn sun, golden and glowing. She hoped to visit China one day. Her mother said it was a beautiful place.

Once she heard her mother talking to her grandmother on Skype. Granny still lived in Xiamen, the city where her mother had grown up. It was on the Eastern coast of China, south of Shanghai and Beijing, close to Taiwan. Her mother would often describe the beaches of Xiamen to Fiona, right after storytime, when she would read out Fiona's favourite fairy tales. The ones by Hans Christian Anderson were her favourites. She particularly liked The Ugly Duckling and The Little Match Girl. Then she would dream about those beaches. China sounded like a wonderful place.

Fiona's eyes moved away from the mirror and downwards to the sky blue carpet that the spiders sometimes ran across, at the bright pink wallpaper adorned with posters of her favourite boy bands, towards her computer desk, where the yellow globules of goo from the lava lamp performed a mystical dance for her. Her laptop was switched off, and there were piles of notepaper, files and text books where homework was in the process of being finished. Then her eyes scanned over to the plug socket in the wall beside her unmade bed. Her phone charger was usually plugged in there, the loose cable running along the carpet like a snake. But it was not there. *Where was it?*

Fiona was about to get up and look for her charger. She would need to pack it in her rucksack ready for the camping trip. She stopped when she heard her little sister running up the stairs and then the inevitable knock on her bedroom door.

'Sisters not allowed', Fiona yelled.

'You've got to finish packing!' Molly insisted. 'Mum says so. She says we are leaving in twenty minutes.'

Fiona got up and went towards the window. Glancing down towards the street in front of the garden, she saw her father putting bags in the boot of their car. He then climbed into the driver's seat and tried to start the engine. It wouldn't start at first, and it took Simon five attempts to get the engine going. *Stupid old car!* Fiona thought. *KNOW*ed the first Princess Spy Diaries game two years ago and she was excited about playing the sequel. Fiona heard Molly go charging back down the stairs to report back to their mother.

Two minutes later Fiona heard Molly's muffled voice in the kitchen. *'She's still playing on her phone. She hasn't packed ANYTHING!'*

When Fiona heard for the third time footsteps on the stairs, she gulped. These footsteps were slower but firmer. Somebody with high-heeled shoes on. This wasn't the baby elephant also known as Molly, this was her mother.

Julie opened the bedroom door and stepped inside. 'Young lady, what have I told you about packing your things?!'

Fiona screwed up her mouth with indignation. 'But I don't want to go camping. And Molly is annoying!'

Julie placed her hands on her hips and sighed. 'We go camping every summer. You will go camping with us and you will jolly well like it! And you need to start being nicer to your sister. She is two years younger than you. You should be looking out for her, and showing her how to do things, like tying her shoelaces, for example. Put that damn phone down at once and pack your things. We're leaving in ten minutes.'

'Molly said it was twenty minutes', Fiona protested.

'We're leaving when I say we're leaving. Now pack your things at once Fiona! I won't ask you again. We need to have a serious talk about your grades too. Maybe if you didn't spend so much time on your phone you'd be doing better at school, like Molly.'

The door slammed shut and Fiona heard her mother's short but firm footsteps retreat down the stairs.

Fiona's head was filled in that moment with many angry thoughts. *I don't like camping. I don't like Molly. I want to stay here with my phone and play Princess Spy Diaries 2. It's not fair!* Fiona was tired of her mother's complaints.

When the dust had cleared, Fiona had a brilliant idea. She stopped looking at the icon for Princess Spy Diaries 2 on her phone. Instead, she pressed the button for Shirley, the phone's robotic assistant.

A big yellow smiley face appeared on the screen. *'Hello Fiona, how can I help you today?'* Shirley said brightly.

With a deep breath, Fiona told Shirley her brilliant plan. *'Shirley, it's Fiona here. I want you to do me a big favour.'*

Fiona waited for her phone to think about her request. Then Shirley said, 'I will certainly try, Fiona. Please, let me know how I can help you?'

Fiona smiled. 'Shirley, I want to go inside my phone.'

'What do you mean?' Shirley asked.

Fiona said, 'I mean, I want to go inside the phone. I want to escape from this world. I don't want to go camping. I don't want to be with my parents or my sister. They are always complaining about me. Fiona, tidy your room, Fiona, feed Whiskers, Fiona, do your homework, Fiona, eat all your sprouts, Fiona, pack your things. I'm sick of it. I wish they would leave me alone but they won't. I want to get away from them. I want to go into my phone.'

There was a long pause as Fiona's smartphone thought about her request. Then Shirley said, 'I don't think that is possible, Fiona. In fact, I think it is impossible.'

Fiona stuck her bottom lip out in frustration. 'Shirley, you cannot be serious?'

Shirley said, 'Do you mean "*Surely, you cannot be serious?*"'

Fiona shook her head solemnly. 'Shirley, I'm serious, I'm really serious. I'm really asking you to do this for me. I want to go inside my phone, away from here.'

Just then, Shirley's bright yellow face winked an eye at Fiona. 'It might be possible. But Fiona, I must tell you, if you do this, then there are three very important rules that you need to know.'

Fiona's face brightened like a Christmas tree. 'Tell me, tell me Shirley! Please, I'll do anything.'

Shirley said, 'Okay, rule number one. If you go inside the phone, you will have to work very hard. It won't be like school, or playing. If somebody wants to use your phone, then you will have to work the apps for them, from the inside. You will basically be the apps. Or, if somebody plays one of your games, you might be one of the characters in the game. You will feel the emotions of that character, like pain or sadness. Do you understand rule number one?'

Fiona thought for a moment. 'Will there be bullies?'

'No', Shirley confirmed, 'there will be no bullies.'

'That sounds reasonable', Fiona decided. 'I can live with that.'

'Okay', Shirley continued, 'then now let me tell you about rule number two. There is only one kind of food or drink inside the phone – electricity. There is no ice cream, no hotdogs, no sweets, no chocolate, no fried chicken, only electricity.'

'What about sprouts?' Fiona enquired.

'Definitely no sprouts', Shirley explained. 'Only electricity'.

'Great!' Fiona exclaimed. 'I mean, I will really miss ice cream, hotdogs, sweets, chocolate and fried chicken. But that's okay, if it means no sprouts. What's rule number three?'

'Rule number three', Shirley began. 'If you play as a character in one of the games, and your character dies, you can never return to the real world. You will die inside the phone.'

Fiona looked again at the notepaper, files and text books on her desk. After the holidays a new school year would start. There would be even more homework, and bigger bullies. This seemed like a good way of escaping from these problems. 'That's okay Shirley, I never want to come back here.'

'Okay, I have now told you all the rules', Shirley said. 'This is a very big decision for you. I think you need some time to consider this carefully.'

Suddenly, a muffled voice interrupted them. It was Julie yelling up from the kitchen. 'Five minutes Fiona. We're leaving in five minutes, with or without you.'

'There's no time to think about it', Fiona scoffed. 'You're going to have to do it now, Shirley, quickly!'

Shirley's smiley face flickered on the phone screen. 'Okay, but I have warned you about the rules. There's no going back once I start the process.'

'JUST DO IT!' Fiona screamed hysterically. 'GET ME AWAY FROM HERE!'

'Okay Fiona, get ready.'

Fiona took a deep breath and sat cross-legged on the sky blue carpet, taking one last long look at her bedroom; at the lava lamp, still dancing, at the boy band posters on her bedroom walls, still smiling warmly at her, at the notepaper and text books, the homework still not getting done any time soon. 'Will this hurt, Shirley?'

'No, it won't hurt, Fiona, but it might feel a bit strange. I have to convert your human body into millions of ones and zeroes.'

'That sounds complicated', Fiona mused.

'Not really', Shirley replied reassuringly. 'Get ready. Prepare yourself. Ten seconds...'

Fiona closed her eyes, clutched her phone tightly to her chest and took one final deep breath. She began to count down from ten to zero like the astronauts had on the television. They had started with a T. T minus 10, 9, 8.... Fiona hadn't known why they had done that. Maybe the T stood for Television? Or perhaps they had just drunk a cup of Tea before the countdown.

As Fiona was going into her phone, she thought it would be a good idea to start with a P. She began to chant, 'P minus 10, 9, 8, 7, 6, 5, 4, 3, 2, 1, ZERO!'

There was a blinding red light and a high pitched noise. Fiona felt like there was a vacuum cleaner droning through her head. The house turned upside down and the ceiling was the floor and the floor was the ceiling. Fiona felt her reality began to stretch, like a giant piece of Blu-Tak. The noise became louder, and the light brighter. And then, all of a sudden, Fiona's bedroom disappeared.

Chapter 2

92% Battery Left

When Fiona opened her eyes she found herself in a large white room. In fact, the room was so large, she could not tell where it started, or ended. It was like a vast, endless tunnel of white. There were no doors, and no windows. The walls were bare – there were no pictures hanging there, and definitely no boy band posters smiling back at her. She was definitely not in her bedroom anymore.

Fiona gathered herself and forced herself to stand. Her ears were ringing and her eyes stung. She remembered what Shirley had told her – Fiona's body had been converted into a digital form. She existed now as a series of zeroes and ones. But as she ran a hand through her long black hair, she realised that she still felt human.

She began to walk around the vast white chamber. Although she could see that her feet were taking steps, the vastness of the white light around her meant that she could not tell if she was actually moving. It was worse than walking through fog. The one difference she did note was that no matter how long she walked, in this world she never felt tired or out of breath.

She walked for what seemed like an eternity, seeing nothing but white. She was supposed to be inside her smartphone, and this was not what she had been expecting.

Her thoughts were interrupted by a low humming noise. It seemed to be very far away, but it was getting gradually louder.

'Hello?' she called out. 'Is anybody there?'

Nothing. Only silence.

'CAN ANYBODY HEAR ME?' she shouted, more loudly this time.

More silence.

The noise grew louder and louder. Fiona stopped dead in her tracks. She began to feel a little frightened. She thought she could see a red flashing light in the distance, lighting up the white canvas for a brief second.

Fiona watched as the red light grew larger. Eventually the silhouette of a grey, metallic object became visible. It was some kind of robot, and it was heading straight for her!

Fiona folded her arms and pinched at her sides with her fingers. This was something she did when she was nervous. She used to do it when the bullies approached her in the school playground. She wondered if this robot coming towards her was also a bully. A smartphone bully! But Fiona reminded herself that Shirley had promised her there were no bullies here.

The robot emerged through the white fog and came to a halt mid-air, hovering in front of her.

'Who are you?' the robot asked. It held a clipboard in a hook that was connected to a metallic arm. The robot glanced at Fiona, then at the clipboard, then back at Fiona. It had red glowing eyes, which flashed slowly every second.

'I'm Fiona', she explained. 'Fiona Chen'.

The robot bleeped, because it couldn't frown. 'You're not on the list of upgrades', it said flatly. 'And we're not expecting a software upgrade until next Tuesday. Are you a virus?'

Fiona thought long and hard. Molly had gotten a virus last winter and had been off school for a whole week. Fiona had to sleep in the spare room because Molly had coughed and spluttered all night long. Her nose had been snotty and she had used up all the tissues. Was this robot now calling Fiona a nasty cold?

'No', Fiona said confidently, 'I am an eight year old girl.'

The robot bleeped again, clearly confused. 'Well, whatever you are, you'll need to come with me. You'll be scanned, processed, and then put to work.'

'Okay', Fiona said, not really understanding what the robot meant. She needed her smartphone's assistant to explain a few things to her. 'Is Shirley here?'

A red laser beam shone from the robot's eye onto the clipboard. After completing its work, the robot looked back at Fiona. 'No, Shirley is somewhere else.'

'What's your name?' Fiona asked the robot.

'My name is Z2134DFY-4', the robot said.

'That's hard to say', Fiona said.

The robot bleeped. 'Well, that's my name.'

'Don't you have a nickname?' Fiona asked.

'A nickname?' the robot asked. 'I don't know what that is.'

'It's a shorter version of your name', Fiona explained. 'Mine is Fi. Or Chenny'.

'Okay', the robot said. More laser beams shone onto the clipboard. 'No, I don't have a nickname.'

'I think I will call you Botty', Fiona decided.

'That's fine', Botty said. 'But we really must go now.'

'How are we getting there?' Fiona asked.

'I'm your bus', Botty explained.

'But you don't look like a bus', Fiona retorted. 'You don't have any wheels.'

'I'm a data bus', Botty explained. 'I take data to where it needs to be. And you my dear are data. So it's time for work. Hop on.'

Botty lowered itself so that it was hovering just below the ground. Reluctantly, Fiona climbed onto its back.

'Hold on tight', Botty said. 'We're going to the Home Screen.'

Fiona had one final question. 'Just to double check, are there any sprouts there Botty?'

The robot flashed its red eyes. 'Sprites? Of course, there are many sprites here, especially in the games.'

Fiona raised an eyebrow in confusion. *Did he say sprites or sprouts?*

'Okay', Fiona said, 'Sprite is fine. I prefer Fanta though. But Shirley told me that I would only have electricity here. Are you sure there is Sprite?'

Botty was no longer listening to her, so she grabbed hold of Botty's robot shoulders as hard as she could. Botty bleeped and whirred and then the white walls around Fiona began to blur and shimmer as Botty picked up speed and whisked her towards the Home Screen.

Chapter 3

89% Battery Left

Fiona opened her eyes several times during the ride, to see the white walls either side of her unchanged. Eventually Botty began to slow down and as Fiona opened her eyes again she began to see swirls of colour fill up the white background around her.

When Botty stopped moving, Fiona instinctively climbed off and rubbed her eyes awake. Her senses tried to take in all the unusual sights and bright colours, but it was quite difficult and Fiona began to feel dizzy. There were so many different colours.

Fiona looked around the large white chamber in front of her. She could see that the floor was organised into large squares and that there were small robots busy working on different tasks in each of the squares. Botty had called this the Home Screen. As Fiona looked closer, she could see signposts in front of each square: Clock, Games, Calendar, Calculator, Email, Chat, Camera, Photos.

Now Fiona knew why this place was called the Home Screen! It was the menu page of her smartphone, and she was right there inside it!

'Do you know what this place is?' Botty enquired.

Fiona nodded. 'Of course.' Fiona's eyes scanned the room again, taking in all the little robots working away to make the apps of her smartphone work properly. Then her eyes moved up to the centre of the chamber. Mounted high up on the white canvas was a large window and from this angle it was too high for Fiona to be able to see anything through it.

Fiona pointed to the window. 'What's up there, Botty?'

Botty followed Fiona's finger and glanced up at the window. 'That's the Viewing Platform', the robot explained. 'It's the portal to the user', it added. 'We can see when a user is about to pick up the phone to start using it. That's where you come in.'

Fiona nodded to herself. 'I am the user', she said to herself, and laughed. 'It's my phone!'

'What did you say?' Botty asked, confused.

Fiona shook her head nonchalantly. 'Er, nothing Botty. So, when the user is asleep, we can relax too?'

Botty shook his robotic head. 'No, we can never rest. There is always work to be done. Even when the user is idle, we can never be idle. Hahahahahaha!' Botty gave a loud, metallic laugh.

Fiona had heard her mother say that her father was idle. Did she mean that he was not moving? Fiona thought that to be idle meant to be lazy, but maybe there was another meaning to the word as well.

Just then, Fiona had an idea. If she could get near the window, she might be able to see her sister and her mother through the Viewing Platform. Fiona had only been inside her phone for a few minutes, but her family would already be angry that they couldn't find her and that she hadn't packed her things for the family trip. *They must be wondering where I am*, Fiona mused. She grinned. *That'll show them!*

'Hey Botty, how do I get up there to see through the window?' Fiona asked.

The robot turned to face her. 'Only higher management have that privilege', he explained. 'You are but a lowly worker. You cannot see through the window.'

'Take me up there, Botty', Fiona insisted. 'I just want to see it once.'

Botty hesitated, but Fiona pleaded with her large brown oval eyes. She even stuck out her bottom lip because that usually worked with her father. 'Please, Botty. Just one look.'

Botty's circuits bleeped and whirred as the robot made a number of risk calculations. 'Okay', the robot said. 'But we will have to be quick. The boss will be here soon, and if she catches us, she will not be happy. You will be deleted and I will be demoted to power on or password recognition duties.'

Fiona smiled. 'Thanks Botty.'

'Well, what are you waiting for?!' Botty exclaimed. 'Climb on. We don't have time for messing around here.'

Fiona climbed back onto Botty and he hovered upwards towards the window. The window sill was a large ledge and Botty landed comfortably onto it. Fiona stepped off, in the same way she stepped off her bike, putting one leg in front of her, which her mother had taught her was a girl's way to do it, and stepped onto the windowsill. Her mother was always telling her to be ladylike, which didn't make any sense to Fiona, as she wasn't yet a lady, she was still a girl.

She peered through the window. At the other side of the glass she could see a small room with boy band posters on the wall. It was her bedroom! Her sister Molly was sat on her bed kicking her feet against the drawers underneath. *Why are you sat on MY bed!* Fiona thought angrily. *You have your own bedroom and your own bed. Get off my bed!* But Fiona did not allow herself to get too angry about it. Instead, she sighed and shrugged and watched as her mother entered her room and her face came close to the window.

'A user is about to pick up the phone', Botty explained.

'You mean my mother?' Fiona asked. Then she regretted it. She realised what she had said but it was too late.

'What did you say?' Botty asked.

'Er, nothing', Fiona said again.

'You are a very strange program', Botty observed. 'As I was saying, a user is about to start using the phone. Look down there at the Home Screen. See all the little bots coming to life on the platform?'

Fiona gazed back down towards the Home Screen, and saw an army of tiny robots preparing themselves on the large coloured squares with military precision.

'Is that what I'm going to be doing, Botty?' Fiona enquired.

'Yes, I have your orders here somewhere. I will give you full instructions in a moment. We need to go back down to the Home Screen now.'

Fiona watched her mother. Her face was a mixture of emotions as she peered down towards the screen. It looked to Fiona like her mother was looking right at her, but Fiona knew that it wasn't possible. Her mother couldn't see her, just like Fiona couldn't see anything extraordinary when she used her phone, except for the app icons. Her mother's face wore expressions of confusion and concern.

Then her father appeared and put his arms around her mother to give her a cuddle. But her mother pulled his arm away. Her father was saying something. Fiona knew this because his lips were moving. But there was no sound, it was just an image. She tried to lip read but her father was speaking too fast and it was too difficult. But Fiona was pretty sure that she had lip-read the last word that her father said before her mother nodded her head in agreement. The word was: *police*.

Fiona smiled. *They really don't know where I am. They are so worried that they must be calling the police. But I'm happy here. I have Botty, and there are no sprouts or bullies here.*

But Fiona could not have been more wrong about that. Her thoughts were broken by a sudden booming noise, like thunder.

'GET DOWN FROM THERE AT ONCE!' a voice boomed from somewhere unseen. 'GET DOWN, OR YOU'LL BE DELETED!' it declared.

The voice was so loud that some of the small robots on the coloured squares below Fiona suddenly exploded. Fiona had to cover her wincing ears, and she cowered backwards further into the windowsill. She sat on the floor and waited for Botty to come and rescue her, but the robot remained rooted to the spot like a statue.

The room appeared to get darker, and Fiona saw shadows beginning to cover the white walls and coloured squares. Whatever had spoken so loudly was clearly very large, and was coming towards Fiona from somewhere.

Frightened, Fiona put her hands over her face and peered forwards through the gaps between her fingers. The room began to vibrate and shake uncontrollably. The footsteps continued and became louder and louder as the shadows on the walls raced faster and faster towards her. Botty was still and silent.

'Botty, what's happening?' Fiona shouted over the noise. Botty did not reply.

Eventually the figure of a giant female robot came into view. It was bigger than anything Fiona had seen in the real world. It was bigger than an aeroplane. It was even bigger than the house where she lived. The robot had a metallic head and body but it was wearing human clothes – a long black dress and red ballerina shoes on eight robotic feet that were as big as cars. It had black lipstick on its metal lips and false eyelashes on its robot head.

The giant robot pointed a giant finger at Fiona, and Fiona flinched. The finger was as large as the bannister on a staircase.

'WHO ARE YOU AND WHAT ARE YOU DOING IN MY PROGRAM?!' The voice was so loud this close to her face. It was like a hurricane and it blew Fiona over. She was now lying down on the windowsill.

'I'm F-f-f-fiona', Fiona stammered. 'F-f-f-fiona Ch-ch-ch-chen.' She was really scared now.

Chapter 4

85% battery left.

Fiona regained her composure and stood up. She looked at Botty, who had been in some kind of robotic trance since this monster had arrived.

'I'm Fiona!' Fiona exclaimed, more confidently. 'Who are you?'

'HAHAHAHAHAHAHAHA' the giant robot roared. 'DON'T YOU KNOW WHO I AM? I AM THE QUEEN! YOUR MASTER! AND YOU ARE MY SLAVE! HAHAHAHAHAHA! AND NOW IT'S TIME FOR YOU TO WORK, LITTLE WORKER!'

'You are speaking to Queen Darkness', Botty confirmed.

Queen Darkness. That sounds familiar! Where do I know that name from? Fiona has in deep thought for a moment.

Queen Darkness then turned towards Botty and pointed her bannister-sized finger at the robot. 'AND YOU! YOU HAVE VIOLATED YOUR PROTOCOLS! TAKING AN UNAUTHORISED PROGRAM TO THE USER VIEWING PLATFORM. I WILL

HAVE TO THINK ABOUT WHAT YOUR PUNISHMENT SHOULD BE!'

Botty's red eyes cast downward and found the edge of the window sill and remained there. Fiona recognised the gesture. Fiona had done the same thing many times when her parents had told her not to pick on her sister or when she hadn't tidied her bedroom or done her homework. For some reason in these moments it was really hard to look them in the eye. Botty had the same reaction to Queen Darkness. Fiona guessed that Botty was just as frightened of her as she was.

'Don't punish him!' Fiona shouted, gaining more confidence from somewhere unknown.

Queen Darkness glared at her. 'HOW DARE YOU TELL ME WHAT TO DO?! THIS IS MY PLATFORM NOW! YOU ARE MY TOY AND YOU WILL DO AS I SAY, NOT THE OTHER WAY AROUND!'

Fiona winced. She had been playing with her toys ever since she could remember. She had controlled them, decided their fate like a God. And now, while she was trapped inside her phone, this huge creature was going to use her like a toy. Suddenly Fiona wondered if this had been a good idea after all.

Fiona glanced back toward the window, where she could still see her family gathered in her bedroom wondering where on earth she was, and how to get her back. Suddenly she looked at her family with a different light in her eyes. A longing. Suddenly Fiona felt scared and alone. But as she watched the faces of her sister, mother and father, she knew that they could not help her now. They couldn't even see her!

Queen Darkness returned her glare towards Botty, who was still rooted to the spot and whirring quietly. 'YOU, DATA BUS! TAKE THIS NAUGHTY PROGRAM AND PUT IT TO WORK ON THE HOME SCREEN!'

Botty nodded without raising its red eyes. 'Which app should I put it to work on, Your Great Majesty?'

Queen Darkness thought for a moment. Then a huge beaming smile appeared across her face, lighting it up like a Christmas tree. 'START IT OFF ON THE CLOCK, AS A SECOND HAND. THAT SHOULD DO FOR THE TIME BEING. LET'S SEE WHAT POTENTIAL SHE HAS. AND DON'T EVER LET ME CATCH YOU UP AT THE USER VIEWING PLATFORM AGAIN WITHOUT

AUTHORISATION, OR YOU WILL BE DELETED. GOT IT?!'

'Yes, your Great Majesty', Botty nodded solemnly.

With a roar and a thunderstorm of electric clicks, Queen Darkness whirled back around to face Fiona. 'I RECOGNISE YOUR BEHAVIOUR FROM SOMEWHERE, PROGRAM. WHERE HAVE I SEEN YOU BEFORE?'

Fiona forced herself to smile, even though she was still very frightened. It seemed that the Queen recognised her, just like she had recognised the Queen. How strange! 'I don't know', she lied.

'HMMMM', Queen Darkness remarked thoughtfully. 'YOU ARE A FAMILIAR PROGRAM TO ME!'

'I'm not a program, I'm an eight year old girl', Fiona tried to explain.

Queen Darkness frowned. 'A GIRL? YOU MEAN, LIKE A USER?'

Fiona wasn't sure how to answer that question. Sometimes she had seen adults on the television get angry at other adults and call them users. But that didn't seem to make sense now. 'I don't know what that is',

Fiona finally uttered, clearing her throat nervously.

'A PROGRAM THAT DOESN'T KNOW WHAT A USER IS?' Queen Darkness barked. 'BAH! I'VE NEVER HEARD OF SUCH A THING! WHAT A MALFUNCTION! PERHAPS YOU NEED A SOFTWARE UPGRADE ALREADY. I SHALL TAKE THAT UNDER ADVISEMENT. NOW, GET TO WORK!'

With that, Queen Darkness turned and stalked off the way she had come from. The buckles on her ballerina shoes rattled as she stalked, without any grace, away from Fiona and Botty. More minions exploded near the Home Screen as she marched down the white corridor and out of sight.

'Come on then', Botty muttered coyly. 'Better get you placed into the clock interface so you can get to work.'

'Botty, who is she and why is she ordering everybody around?'

Botty squeaked and whirred. 'It's a long story. Hop on and I'll take you to the clock.'

Fiona clambered aboard Botty and held on tight again, clinging on for dear life, as Botty took flight away from the giant window ledge and down towards the Home Screen.

Fiona glanced back at the window and took in a final glimpse of her family members. They were still huddled on her bed looking sad and doubtful.

Chapter 5

82% Battery Left

Botty landed in the Home Screen on a large green platform next to a big sign that read, 'Clock'. Fiona hopped off and watched as tiny minion robots scurried around with tiny clipboards, performing jobs and checking that everything was running smoothly.

'It was mean to start you on the Clock', Botty observed.

'Why do you say that?' Fiona enquired.

'Well, some apps only require work to be done on them when the user makes contact. These are reactive apps. But the clock is a proactive app. Even when the user is not there, time keeps on ticking. It needs to be continuous, so that when the user does make contact, the time on the display is correct. Do you understand?'

Fiona nodded. 'Like my watch. It's always ticking, even when I'm not looking at it.' Fiona looked at her arm but it was bare. She'd forgotten to put on her watch that morning. She had no idea what time it was.

A few of the minion robots approached and Botty began squeaking orders at them.

Fiona was curious, 'What happens now, Botty? How does this work?'

'You heard Her Majesty', Botty explained. 'You are going to be the second hand of the clock app. We need to attach you to the clock'.

Fiona nodded again. 'Where is the clock?'

Botty pointed to a spot behind Fiona. She followed the direction of his robotic finger and turned around to face the opposite direction. There was a giant circular structure in front of her, painted black. It had a long thin tower reaching upwards from the left side of the dome. It was so large that Fiona had to take a step back to take it all in. It was then when she realised that the structure was a giant number 6. She could make out other, faint structures either side of it.

'The 5 and the 7', Botty explained, reading her mind.

'It's massive!' Fiona exclaimed.

'Yes it is', Botty agreed. 'So you will have to climb on board again because I need to attach you to the top.'

'Okay', Fiona said, reluctantly. She had hoped that being in her phone was going to be more fun than this! But that was before she knew that Queen Darkness was pulling the strings. Shirley had clearly told her that there were no bullies in this world, and yet Queen Darkness seemed like the biggest bully in the whole universe. She made the bullies in the school playground look like irrelevant dust mites by comparison.

With Fiona once again clinging on for dear life, Botty flew upwards towards the top of the giant clock. As he ascended, Fiona was astonished to find two small girls inside the clock. One of them was absolutely still, like a statue, and the other one moved slightly. She met their eyes and waved to them. They waved back hesitantly. They had concerned and tired looks on their faces.

'Who are they?' Fiona asked.

'The minute hand and the hour hand', Botty explained. 'Your colleagues.'

'What's a colleague?' Fiona asked.

'The people that you work with', Botty explained. 'You're a very basic program, aren't you?!'

Fiona shook her head emphatically. 'I already told you. I'm not a program, I'm an eight year old girl. Hey, the minute hand and the hour hand, they look like me!'

'I cannot explain why that is', Botty murmured awkwardly.

'Why not, Botty?' Fiona asked.

'I am not programmed to know about such things. My job is to transport programs from A to B.'

Fiona snorted. 'Well, now who's a basic program, eh Botty? Hahahahaha.'

They landed at the top of the clock and docked on a giant platform beside two large black structures. One was a vertical skyscraper with no special features, just a block. The structure to its right had more curves in it. Fiona looked closely at the two structures and realised that they were a giant 1 and a giant 2. Together they represented a giant 12.

More minion robots appeared, squeaking and squawking and driving in circles around Fiona. Botty watched as they hoisted her up onto the top of the platform, using winches and wires. Fiona was wearing a baggy pink sweater. One of the minion robots hooked the back of her sweater onto a winch.

'Remember', Botty explained, 'You are the second hand. You have to move slightly around the clock every second, for a total of sixty times. Every sixtieth time you will come back to this position under the 12. The minute hand will move slightly. You will do the whole thing sixty times, so you will be moving three thousand six hundred times every hour. After you have done that, the hour hand will move to the next number. The three of you must repeat this process over and over again, without stopping, without failing, to keep the time correct.'

Fiona tried to do the maths in her head, but maths wasn't her best subject. She preferred History. Molly was really good at maths.

'You might feel a bit dizzy at first', Botty explained, 'But you'll get used to it.'

'What happened to the last second hand?' Fiona asked.

'You don't want to know the answer to that question', Botty remarked. 'But let me tell you that something happened, and Queen Darkness got very angry. You don't want that to happen now do you?'

Fiona gulped. 'No.'

'Right', Botty declared. 'Better get you started before a user appears. If they detect that the time has been stopped for several minutes now, there might be problems. Quick. Get her started.'

One of the minions flicked a switch on the wall and the winch kicked into action. Fiona began to spin slowly around the clock.

Chapter 6

80% Battery Left

As Fiona began to spin slowly around the clock, she began to wonder who the other two girls were. The statuesque girl was positioned under the giant number 10. She was the hour hand. She had black skin and her hair was in braids. She was wearing a bright red sweater, pink jeans and purple trainers. The other girl, who moved every minute, was currently stood under the giant 7. She had short black hair and brown skin. She was wearing a long yellow sari and green sandals. Both girls were very pretty, and Fiona wanted to befriend them.

By looking at the positions of the girls under the giant numbers Fiona calculated the current time to be 10:35 a.m. Which made sense. It meant that she had been inside her phone for about an hour. Fiona realised that she would only get a short window of opportunity to speak to both girls every minute, because after a few seconds she would be spinning around the clock and away from them. She would then have to wait another minute each time. So she would have to speak fast and loudly.

After 35 seconds she reached the girl in the yellow sari. 'Hi, I'm Fiona', she shouted. She was upside down and her hair flopped over her face. She couldn't see anything! 'What are you doing here?' she added.

'I'm Sunita', the girl shouted back. 'I recognise you but I think we go to different schools. I've seen you playing outside before'. *Sunita, what a nice name,* Fiona thought. Like a miniature version of the sun.

Fiona realised that Sunita hadn't answered her question about why she was there. She would have to wait another minute now. How frustrating! She continued to spin around the second half of the clock.

When she reached the number 10 she shouted to the girl with the braids. 'Hi, I'm Fiona', she repeated. 'What are you doing here?' she repeated.

'My name is Sharlene', the girl shouted back. 'We asked Shirley to send us here because we thought it would be fun', Sharlene explained. *Sharlene – another lovely name!*

'Me too!' Fiona called out. But before she could say more, Sharlene disappeared from view and Fiona made her way back towards her starting position by the giant 12. It was so annoying to have to talk like this, one quick question and answer at a time.

On the second spin Fiona anxiously waited for her opportunity to speak with Sunita again. Another minute had passed so Sunita had moved slightly towards the number 8. Eventually the seconds ticked by and Sunita's upside down form came into view.

'How long have you been here?' Fiona called out.

'About six months', Sunita called back, excitedly. 'It's so exciting to see a new face! And a human face at that! All I see these days is a clock face, robots, and, if I'm lucky, Sharlene. Oh, and HER, the one they call the Queen.'

'Six months!' Fiona exclaimed, horrified. 'That must have been hell. And you've always been on this clock, or were you in other apps too?'

Sunita disappeared through the gap between Fiona's hair as she moved around the clock towards Sharlene.

When Fiona reached the number 10, she caught a better glimpse of Sharlene than last time. Fiona guessed that Sunita's family were probably from India and Sharlene's from Africa.

'No, we've been moved around a lot', Sharlene spoke first. 'But we were put here a month ago by Queen Darkness as punishment for being naughty. My arms and legs ache. It's hard being the hour hand – you have to keep so still all the time.' Sharlene wriggled her body against the wires that kept her in place to try and get some air into her muscles.

'The easiest job was the alarm clock', Sunita explained. 'All you had to do was make a loud noise once every morning!'

'The best job was being the camera', Sharlene shared. 'Because you got to see the outside world again. I could see the park, and my friend's dog, and my bedroom.'

Fiona started to speak but Sharlene had already disappeared and she found herself back at the 12. *This is going to be exhausting,* Fiona mused. *But at least I have made two nice new friends!*

On the third rotation around the giant clock, Fiona reached Sunita, who had moved another few feet towards the number 8. 'It was Shirley's idea', Sunita said solemnly. 'And I couldn't resist.'

Shirley! Fiona had forgotten all about Shirley. 'Yes, we need to speak to Shirley', she decided. 'She lied to us. How can we summon her?'

Fiona knew that Sunita wouldn't have time to answer, but Sharlene would.

When Fiona reached 10, Sharlene said, 'We're not sure. But if we all shout her name loud enough, surely she will come?'

Fiona thought about that while she rotated past Sharlene and onwards towards Sunita. But how would they co-ordinate it between the three of them?

When Fiona arrived by Sunita, she was about to ask the question, but it seemed that Sunita had read her mind. 'It needs to be at a time when the three of us are the closest distance from each other. That way we can channel our voices and project them as one. Tell Sharlene.'

Fiona nodded and when she reached Sharlene she relayed the message.

'Good thinking', Sharlene agreed. 'So let's calculate it.'

Fiona wasn't very good at maths, but she reckoned that she could figure this out. As she span slowly towards Sunita, she did the calculations in her head. It was now 10:38.

Sharlene wasn't going to be moving for another 22 minutes, and even then it wouldn't be far. So the best idea was for Fiona and Sunita to both be as close to the number 10 as possible. For Sunita, that would be another 21 minutes, at 10:59, when Sunita would be just a few feet away. For Fiona, it would be on the 59th second.

When Fiona reached Sunita, they both smiled and at the same time shouted, '10:59!' They had calculated the answer at the same time. When Fiona reached Sharlene, the same thing happened. Sharlene said '10:59' at the same time as Fiona did. So they had to wait another twenty minutes.

By the end of the twenty minutes Fiona was beginning to feel dizzy from all the spinning. As she made her way around the clock at 10:59 she could see that Sunita and Sharlene had now lined up into position. The seconds brought her ever closer. At 10:59 and 55 seconds, Fiona readied herself. 'After 3', she shouted. '1, 2, 3 – NOW!'

'SHIRLEY!!!!!!!!!!!' the three girls shouted at the top of their lungs.

Nothing seemed to happen. Fiona then began to move away from the other two girls again. *It didn't work,* Fiona guessed. She felt downhearted. She glanced at Sunita and Sharlene and saw the dismay on their faces. But then after another minute, at 11 o'clock exactly, when Fiona once again became near Sunita and Sharlene, a large yellow face appeared on the wall. But this time it wasn't smiling. It had a horizontal black line for a mouth.

Chapter 7

77% Battery Left

'Hello', Shirley said flatly. 'How can I help you today?'

'Oh, I think you know how you can help us today!' Fiona snorted equally as flatly. But then she began to move away from Shirley and her new friends, as she moved slowly around the clock once more.

A frown appeared across Shirley's face. 'Please be more specific', Shirley uttered in a shrill tone. 'I don't understand your request.'

And then Sharlene had an idea. 'Don't say it', Sharlene said to Shirley. 'Fiona won't hear you. Can you write it instead?'

The face on the wall blinked and text began to appear on the bare white wall in front of the clock. PLEASE BE MORE SPECIFIC. I DO NOT UNDERSTAND YOUR REQUEST. Fiona read the words upside down as she passed the 6 and then slowly began to correct herself as she approached the 12.

When she approached the 12, she shouted, 'Shirley! What's going on? I thought being inside the phone was going to be fun?!'

Fiona read Shirley's response as she rotated around the clock. I DID EXPLAIN THE RULES. AND I DID WARN YOU THAT YOU WOULD HAVE TO WORK HARD.

When Fiona reached 12 again, it was Sunita's turn to contribute. 'Yes, but you didn't tell us about Queen Darkness or that we would be her slaves. You didn't explain that there was a bully in here who would control us like this. You said no bullies, Shirley!!!'

I'M SORRY GIRLS, IT WAS HER MAJESTY, SHE MADE ME DO IT.

One minute later, when Fiona was back in an upright position, she said, 'What does she want with us?'

The girls waited patiently for Shirley's response. Then it came. Three small words, which didn't help the girls at all.

I DON'T KNOW.

There was a long pause. Then, more words appeared on the white wall.

SOMETHING HAPPENED. SHE IS A VERY POWERFUL PROGRAM. SHE TOOK CONTROL OF EVERYTHING ON THE HOME SCREEN. AND ME OF COURSE. CLEARLY SHE WANTS

SOMETHING WITH YOU, AND SHE LIKES TO HUMILIATE CHILDREN.

By this point Fiona was back at 12, but Sunita was starting to slip away as she moved the minutes of time forward and began heading towards the giant 1.

'But', Fiona started, 'This is my phone! Why are Sunita and Sharlene here? Shouldn't they be trapped inside their own phones?'

I DO NOT KNOW THE ANSWER TO THIS QUESTION. I'VE ALREADY TOLD YOU TOO MUCH. I SHOULD GO NOW. IF HER MAJESTY DISCOVERS THAT I HAVE BEEN TALKING TO YOU, SHE WILL DESTROY ME.

'She can't destroy you', Fiona protested. 'You're the phone's personal assistant. We need you! The users need you.'

YOU DON'T KNOW HER POWERS. YOU SHOULD NEVER UNDERESTIMATE HER.

'Shirley, you have to help us escape from here!' Sunita exclaimed.

Fiona thought about that for a moment. She had been brought to the Home Screen from the place where she first arrived by Botty. Botty was their best way to escape back to that place, and then back to the real world. But where was Botty?

I'M SORRY. I CAN'T. I HAVE TO GO NOW BEFORE A PROGRAM DISCOVERS ME HERE TALKING TO YOU.

'Please Shirley, you must help us', Sharlene protested. 'We don't belong here. We miss the real world. We miss our friends and our family and our toys.'

Shirley's horizontal mouth changed to a semi-circular curve, indicating a sad face. Then the yellow face disappeared from the white wall altogether. Shirley was gone.

Chapter 8

70% Battery Left

It was now 12:30 and the girls had continued to spin around the clock in their given roles, talking about what to do.

'Even if we manage to get these straps off, we would plunge to our deaths', Sunita declared.

'It's a long way to fall', Sharlene agreed.

'It's impossible!' Fiona screamed. 'We're doomed. We'll be here forever!'

'If we could just find a way to loosen the wires enough to slip underneath them...' Sunita started.

'But we'll fall!' Fiona protested.

'Not if we time it perfectly', Sharlene revealed.

'What do you mean?' Fiona asked.

'At exactly 10:50 tonight, a large robot will fly past us, underneath the clock', Sharlene explained.

Fiona wondered where she was going with this. 'And?'

'And', Sharlene continued, 'if we find a way to loosen the straps we could slip underneath them and land on the robot.'

'How do you know about the robot and the exact time it passes?' Fiona asked.

'Because it passes underneath us at exactly that time every single day', Sunita answered.

'The timing would have to be perfect though', Sharlene offered. 'If we misjudge it, we would miss the robot. We'd fall and die.'

'Where does the robot go?' Fiona enquired.

'We have no idea', Sunita said.

'It's a chance we'd have to take', Sharlene added.

'I still don't understand why you two are here', Fiona muttered, 'if this is my phone.'

Sunita and Sharlene frowned, and for a moment looked dejected.

'I'm sorry', Fiona said. 'I didn't mean to sound mean. I mean, I'm glad you are here with me.'

They all smiled, which made them forget their predicament for a few seconds.

Then Fiona had an idea. While strapped to the clock her hands were held down by her sides, but if she wriggled she could just about get her left hand inside her left jeans pocket, where she kept her hair comb. It was an old comb and some of the bristles had broken off. The remaining bristles had been slowly worn thinner into sharp points. Fiona used to use it in her lunch break at school to cut her sandwiches into smaller pieces. It was a comb, but it was also a knife.

Fiona dug deep into her pocket and felt the tips of the bristles. She hoped the sharp ones would not cut her fingers. 'Girls, I have an idea.'

She wriggled forcefully and stretched her fingers as far as they would go. Eventually she felt them make contact with the comb and she pulled it out of her pocket. Then she explained to her two new friends what they had to do.

'We can use this comb to cut the straps', Fiona explained. 'We don't need to cut them off completely, or we will fall. But we can cut them enough so that we can slip underneath them when the time comes.'

Sunita and Sharlene liked Fiona's plan very much and the three girls began to get excited about what could happen later that day, when 10:50 p.m. came around, when the transport bot would be flying underneath them – their getaway vehicle.

'I'll cut my own straps first', Fiona explained further. 'Then, when I get as close to Sunita as possible, I will throw the comb to Sunita. Sunita, you must catch it! If you drop the comb, our plan fails'.

Sunita nodded in understanding. 'I won't drop it, I promise. Then I will cut my straps a bit. After that, I will throw it to Sharlene.'

'And I will catch it and then do the same', Sharlene declared.

'Great!' Fiona said.

Sunita said, 'Fiona, did your Mum buy your phone brand new from a shop or was it second-hand?'

Fiona thought about that for a second. 'I don't know. Why do you ask?'

'Well', Sunita explained, 'It might explain why we're all here in the same phone. Maybe it was my phone before it was yours. And maybe it was Sharlene's before it was mine.'

'It's possible', Fiona thought out aloud.

As the hours wore on, and the girls moved around the clock, they chatted and got to know each other better. They talked about their favourite toys and music, about the bullies at school, the teachers they liked and their best and worst subjects. Sharlene was really good at maths. Sunita's strongest subject was science. Fiona really liked history. None of them liked bullies, and they all agreed that Queen Darkness was the biggest bully they had ever had the misfortune of meeting!

At 10:00 p.m., with fifty minutes to go before the transport bot would appear, Fiona set to work on her straps. There were four in total – one for each arm and one for each leg. She worked with the comb, scratching at the strips of nylon holding her together. At first it didn't appear to be working, and she looked at Sunita's upside down frame in a panic as she passed by her.

'Keep trying', Sunita shouted, understanding the look on Fiona's face. 'Don't give up!'

Fiona sawed and sawed and sawed, frantically, and eventually the edges of the nylon strap began to fray. Fiona giggled with a new excitement. 'It's working!' she shouted triumphantly.

Fiona sawed some more and eventually her right arm loosened up a little as the nylon strap frayed even more. Now she could move her arm. It was so sore and stiff from being attached to the clock for so long. She had to wriggle her arm around to get the circulation back into it. She did the same with the other arm, which then allowed her

to bend forward and reach down to her waist
to begin sawing at the straps on her legs. It
took her another ten minutes.

'Okay, I am finished. Sunita, are you ready
for the comb?'

'I'm ready', Sunita yelled back confidently.

Fiona span around the clock until she saw
Sunita's small frame superimposed against
the giant number 4. It was now 10:20 p.m.
Here goes! Fiona thought. *Don't drop it
Sunita!*

Fiona threw the comb and her heart
skipped a beat as the comb flew through
mid-air and on towards Sunita, whose eyes
were wide with anticipation and
concentration. The comb passed Sunita's
face and into the funnel that she had made
by cupping her hands together.

'YES!' they screamed in unison. Fiona
clapped her hands, the only one of them able
to do so. But that would soon change. Sunita
looked at the comb, as Fiona watched from
her rotations around the clock.

'You see where it's sharp in the middle?'
Fiona yelled. 'Just use it like a saw,
backwards and forwards.' Fiona had
watched her Dad cutting wood with a large
saw in their family garage before. They used

the wood to feed the coal fire in winter. It was how she had known how to saw at the nylon straps.

Sunita nodded and then set to work, using the same technique that Fiona had used. After ten more minutes, at 10:30 p.m., Sunita was free enough from the straps to be able to slide underneath them when the time was right.

'Sharlene, it's all on you now!' Sunita shouted.

'No pressure then!' Sharlene replied sarcastically.

It was 10:30 p.m. Sharlene was stood under the giant 10 like a statue. Sunita was at the 3. Sunita knew that Sharlene was too far away from her. Sunita was a fielder in school rounders, and she was really good at it. But even with her skills she knew that she couldn't possibly throw the comb all the way over to the number 10 from the number 3.

As if reading her mind, Fiona said, 'Sunita, you'll have to throw it back to me. Then I'll throw it to Sharlene when I reach her.'

'Got it', Sunita replied.

'Wait for me to get close to you', Fiona demanded. Fiona then span around the clock until she reached Sunita. She threw the comb and it hit Fiona on the cheek. As it bounced off her cheek Fiona reached out and grabbed it with one hand. 'Got it', she confirmed.

'Wahoo!' Sharlene yelled excitedly.

'Sharlene, it's 10:35 now', Fiona declared matter-of-factly. 'We are running out of time. Are you ready?'

'I was born ready!' Sharlene yelled back.

'What does that mean?' Fiona asked.

'I don't know', Sharlene replied. 'But some guy said it on the TV once.'

'Okay, well here it comes, Born Ready', Fiona said. As she passed the giant number 10 Fiona tossed the comb in Sharlene's direction.

As the comb neared Sharlene's reach, time seemed to slow down into a painful slow motion. Fiona and Sunita looked on with bated breath. Sharlene reached out with her hand and the comb bounced off it, continuing on its path through the air, directed by gravity and its own weight, away from Sharlene.

Sunita cupped her hand over her mouth with worry and Fiona placed both hands on the top of her head and closed her eyes.

Sharlene raised her other hand, and the comb bounced off that one too, once, twice, three times, then finally came to rest on Sharlene's upturned palms.

When Fiona opened her eyes, she heard Sunita gasp and then she looked at Sharlene, who had a horrified expression on her face. Nevertheless, Sharlene was clutching the comb in the palm of her hand like it was her baby.

'That was a close one', Sunita observed.

'Too close', Fiona muttered.

Then Sharlene began to saw like crazy.

Fiona said, 'Sharlene, it's 10:45. We have five minutes left before the transport bot arrives. You'll have to loosen your straps a lot faster than we did.'

'I know I know! I'm doing it as fast as I can', Sharlene protested.

Sharlene sawed ferociously at all four straps holding her to the clock. Because she was the hour hand, and hadn't moved for a while, and was now perfectly still, she had the advantage. She did not feel dizzy and she could saw more efficiently. She concentrated furiously and sawed and sawed and sawed until the frayed straps loosened and loosened and then she felt a little jolt as her body moved slightly. Then she put Fiona's comb into her pocket.

'Okay, I've done it', Sharlene declared proudly. 'Girls, we are ready to get out of here!'

'Okay, at precisely 10:50, when that transport bot comes, we'll all be as close together as we can be', Sunita explained. 'Sharlene will be under the 10, I'll be under the 10, and Fiona, you'll be under the 12.'

Even though Fiona could calculate the exact time of day by looking at the position of her body, and Sunita and Sharlene's bodies, Fiona had no concept of day or night inside the smartphone. All she saw was the stark white walls, ceiling and floor. It never changed. A whole day had now passed since Fiona escaped from her real life and into this virtual one. She thought about her parents and her sister. They must be going out of their minds with worry by now. Fiona wondered if they had called the police yet, and officially reported her as a missing person. And then she thought about Sunita's family, and Sharlene's. Her two friends had been inside the phone a lot longer than her. By now their families must have decided that their little girls had gone forever. How terrible! For a moment Fiona felt really sad.

Then Fiona suddenly remembered that this was not the time for worrying. She had to be focused. They were about to make a daring escape.

At 10:50 p.m. the transport bot arrived, right on schedule.

'NOW!' Sharlene yelled.

In the same instant all three girls slid underneath their frayed straps – the shackles that had kept them enslaved and prisoners of the clock.

Fiona gulped as she felt the rush of a sudden vertical drop. It must have felt like the rollercoasters that the older girls at school talked about. It must have been the same feeling. They seemed to be falling forever, sheer white all around them.

As Fiona looked down, trying not to scream, the transport bot came into view.

Fiona felt a crash as she made impact with something. She heard two more crashing sounds and hoped it was her friends landing on the bot as well. It looked a little like Botty but it wasn't Botty.

Fiona glanced behind her and saw Sunita and Sharlene clutching tightly around the bot's metal wings. Fiona had landed on the main body of the transport bot. She glanced upwards and watched the giant clock slowly disappear from view as the giant numbers became smaller and smaller. It was odd to see the clock from this angle. It was like looking at a clock the normal way, in the real world. The real world that Fiona suddenly missed, and longed for.

Chapter 9

64% Battery Left

The clock disappeared entirely from view as the transport bot that looked a bit like Botty carried them through the body of Fiona's smartphone. Steadying herself, Sharlene slithered across the bot's body like a snake, towards the wing where Fiona was hanging on for dear life.

'Take my hand', Sharlene said. She reached out and Fiona grabbed her hand. With all her might, Sharlene heaved and pulled and dragged Fiona onto the safety of the bot's body.

'Thanks', Fiona said. 'You are very strong, Sharlene'.

Smiling at the compliment, Sharlene did the same thing with Sunita, who had landed on the opposite wing and had also been clinging tightly to it.

The three girls were now lying side by side, watching the white walls twitch and glimmer all around them as they moved at high speed. It was strange for Fiona to see the other two girls up close, and not tied to the clock. It was also the first time that she had seen Sunita the right way up, not upside down as she had been when Fiona had been spinning around the clock.

'Do we know where we are going?' Fiona asked.

'No idea', Sunita declared.

'There should be a destination written somewhere on the bot', Sharlene explained.

Fiona frowned. 'How come you know so much about this place?'

'I've been here a long time', Sharlene said sullenly.

'This phone must have been yours originally', Fiona guessed. 'Your parents must have bought it new from a shop. How long have you been here exactly?'

'Almost two years', Sharlene said.

'Wow. So you missed two Christmasses and two birthdays? You didn't get any presents for two years? I can't imagine it! That's horrible!'

'Yes, but there are other things I have missed more', Sharlene explained. 'Ice cream, TV, our garden, my Mum.'

'Hmmmmm', Fiona said thoughtfully. 'I didn't think I could possibly miss my Mum, but actually I do, and I've only been here a day. What about you Sunita? How long have you been here?'

'About six months', Sunita answered. 'When I first got the phone for my birthday, it had a red sticker on the back.'

'Oh my God!' Sharlene exclaimed. 'I put that sticker there!'

'It seems like you are right about the phone being second hand to us', Sunita said to Fiona. 'I added a yellow sticker underneath.'

'YES!' Fiona shouted. 'When I got the phone it had a red sticker and a yellow sticker on the back! I added my own, a green sticker. How funny!'

'That explains it', Sharlene stated.

'Well, not exactly', Fiona said. 'It doesn't explain how it's possible for us to be here, or how that huge horrible monster is able to do this to us! I'm sure I've seen that thing before somewhere.'

'Us too', Sunita said. 'But we can't remember where from, right Sharlene?'

'Right', Sharlene nodded her agreement.

'Here, I found it', Fiona said, looking at a small black screen on the bot's back. There were red letters moving across it like the screens at the train station that displayed the places the trains stop at. 'It says that we are going back to the Home Screen.'

'That's not good', Sharlene explained. 'If we go back there, we'll be caught by Queen Darkness and put back to work somewhere. Probably the clock again. Or whatever amuses her the most. We have to try to change the bot's destination so we can go somewhere else to hide.'

'I have an idea', Fiona declared. 'My phone has a memo app.'

'Don't you mean, *our* phone', Sharlene corrected.

'Well yes, I suppose technically it is *our* phone', Fiona realised. 'Okay, our phone has a memo app. If we can find a way to hack into the memo app, we can write a message which hopefully my family will see. We can tell them that we are alive but we need their help. They can then show it to the police and they will help us.'

'It's a good plan', Sunita declared.

'It might work', Sharlene added. 'But isn't there a password protecting your phone? Will they be able to get into your phone to see any new messages?'

Fiona snorted. 'Yes, I have a pattern on mine. You have to make an F shape. F for

Fiona, haha. But I know my little sister Molly knows it, because I've seen her peering over the top of our bunk bed when I'm below her, and I know she has seen me use my pattern.'

'She's your little sister, and she got the top bunk?' Sunita snorted. 'There's no way I would allow that!'

'Me neither!' Sharlene agreed. 'No way!'

'My parents made me do it. They said I should be nicer to my little sister so she got the top bunk. When my mother was growing up in China they had very little. They were so poor, they could only afford to eat rice once or twice a year. Can you imagine that? We are very lucky now, so my mother wants me to respect my sister. I don't mind so much. On the bottom bunk I can get to the bathroom before her!'

'Well that's true', Sunita agreed. 'My grandparents had the same problems in India'.

'And mine in Africa', Sharlene added.

'Okay, so the memo app is on the home screen', Sharlene said, bringing the conversation back to their plan.

'But like we just said, we can't just go back there, we'll be caught and punished', Sunita replied.

'So what can we do?' Fiona asked. 'We need a disguise.'

'I wonder if there is a way to re-program this transport bot?' Sunita thought out loud.

'Can we get inside it?' Sharlene wondered.

'Look, there's a hatch', Fiona declared. She pointed to the front of the bot near its head. The three girls crawled over to it. The hatch was a square about the size of a sink. Fiona tried the handle but it didn't budge. 'It looks heavy', she said. 'It's not moving.'

'Let me try', Sunita offered. She wrapped both hands around the handle and heaved with all her might. The hatch still didn't budge.

'Can I have a go?' Sharlene asked. Fiona and Sunita moved aside as Sharlene put her left hand on the hatch handle and heaved. There was a scraping noise, and then finally, the hatch lid came apart in her hand.

'Wow!' Fiona observed. 'You really are strong!'

They peered inside the hatch. All they could see was a dark tunnel.

'Ready?' Fiona said.

'You first', Sharlene replied.

Fiona took a deep breath, not knowing what to expect once she entered the bot's belly. Would there be more monsters inside? More surprises? Well, Fiona thought, if there were more monsters, they would be small ones. A lot smaller than Queen Darkness to be able to fit inside the transport bot, that's for sure.

Fiona didn't like dark tunnels or small spaces. When she was four years old she had been playing in the garden and she had fallen into a hole between the wall and the road. She had been trapped there for hours before her parents had found her. Ever since then she had been scared of small, dark holes. Whenever she got off a train and saw the *Mind The Gap* sign, she would shudder as if in an icy chasm. Fiona could not show her new friends that she was scared now, or they might make fun of her.

'Okay', Fiona stated firmly. 'I'm going in.'

She slithered through the hatch into the tunnel, and soon after that, her friends followed. Then the hatch door closed with a loud boom, and everything was black.

Chapter 10

60% Battery Left

Fiona blinked as her eyes adjusted to the darkness. Small red lights on the ceiling of the narrow tunnel provided some light. She crawled along the tunnel and eventually it opened out into a small chamber. She was in the belly of the bot now.

Sunita and Sharlene emerged behind her. There were no windows in the chamber. There was writing on all the walls though. Fiona looked at it. It was a series of numbers. Fiona felt her stomach tighten with dread. She hated maths!

'Equations', Sharlene explained. 'Code. It must be the bot's instructions.'

'You mean, like, where it has to go. Like a taxi?' Sunita offered.

'Exactly', Sharlene replied. 'This is what we need', she added, pointing to a computer mounted on the wall in the far corner of the chamber. Its screen was black, and Fiona thought that perhaps it was switched off.

'I understand basic code', Sunita said. She pressed her finger on the monitor and it whirred to life. A small yellow smiley face appeared. 'How can I help you?' it stated robotically.

'Shirley! Oh my god! Is that you?' Fiona exclaimed.

'No, I am not Shirley', the smiley face replied. 'What do you want?'

'I'll handle this', Sunita declared, pushing the other girls aside. She asked the smiley face for a keyboard and after a few seconds a keyboard appeared on the monitor. Touching the screen, Sunita began to type out commands that neither Sharlene nor Fiona understood.

'You are very smart', Fiona observed.

'I have to be. My parents want me to be a doctor when I grow up. Just give me a few more seconds', Sunita said. 'Here, I've got it. I'm in the Memo app now. What message do you want to write?'

Fiona thought about that for a moment. She wondered if her family or the police could really help them. Was this a waste of time? No! She forced herself to stay positive.

'Okay, type this', Fiona ordered.

DEAR FAMILY,
IT'S ME, FIONA! I'M ALIVE! I'M TRAPPED INSIDE MY PHONE. THIS IS

NOT A JOKE, I AM NOT MESSING AROUND. DON'T ASK ME HOW THAT IS POSSIBLE – I DON'T KNOW! I DIDN'T WANT TO GO TO THE LAKE DISTRICT AND I THOUGHT IT WOULD BE FUN TO BE INSIDE MY PHONE. BUT IT'S NOT, NOT AT ALL! I AM BEING WORKED LIKE A SLAVE. AND THERE IS A HUGE MONSTER, A BIG BULLY, WHO IS CONTROLLING ME. ALSO, THERE ARE TWO OTHER GIRLS IN HERE. SUNITA SINGH AND SHARLENE MUTUKA. TELL THEIR FAMILIES THE SAME. WE ARE TRYING TO ESCAPE BUT YOU MUST HELP US. WE DON'T KNOW HOW TO GET OUT. THE PASSWORD PATTERN ON MY PHONE IS AN F SHAPE, IF YOU DIDN'T ALREADY KNOW (I KNOW MOLLY KNOWS!). ALSO, PLEASE MAKE SURE YOU CHARGE MY PHONE EVERY DAY. IF THE BATTERY DIES, WE DIE IN HERE! PLEASE HURRY! OH, AND MUM? I'M SORRY, I MISS YOU, I LOVE YOU. FIONA.

'Okay, it's finished. You can send it', Fiona said.

'That's a good message', Sharlene shared.

'I hope it works', Fiona declared with a sigh.

'Message sent', Sunita confirmed, flicking a loose tuft of hair back behind her ear with a flourish.

Sharlene scratched her head. 'Okay, this map shows where we are. It looks like we are getting close to the Home Screen. We need to find a way to change the destination, we need to find a place to hide while we think about our next move. Sunita, can you do that?'

'I think so', Sunita answered. 'Let me try.'

Sunita began typing on the keyboard again.

Fiona looked at Sharlene. 'Now what?'

'I really don't know!' Sharlene said.

They sat down on the smooth tiled floor inside the belly of the transport bot, putting their hands up to their ears and their knees up to their chins as they thought about how to escape from the phone, about how to escape from Queen Darkness.

All of a sudden their thoughts were interrupted by a loud crashing sound, like thunder. The force of something threw Sunita away from the computer and she landed awkwardly on the floor with a thud. Fiona's heart nearly jumped out of her skin. Sharlene looked similarly dazed.

It took a few seconds for Fiona's mind to come around from its slumber. 'What happened?' she whispered, but she didn't think her friends had heard her. Her head felt groggy and she thought she might throw up. But somehow she didn't.

As the air cleared of the thunder, the hatch door opened, and a strange foul smell drifted down into the tunnel. It was like stale sprouts, and Fiona had to cover her mouth. She looked at Sharlene and saw her nose wrinkle. Sunita was just about picking herself up off the floor.

'I know what that smell is', Sharlene uttered sombrely. 'It's HER.'

'Who?' Fiona asked. But she already knew the answer. She gazed up at the giant, ugly face gazing angrily down at them. QUEEN DARKNESS! She had caught the transport bot in one of her giant hands.

The Queen said nothing. She just pointed a giant finger at Fiona, and shook her head. Every time she breathed out, the tunnel filled up with the smell of stale sprouts.

'She's got us now!' Sunita squeaked.

'THAT'S RIGHT, I DO!' Queen Darkness roared. 'YOU'D BETTER COME OUT OF THERE RIGHT NOW, OR I WILL DESTROY YOU!'

'What do we do now?' Sharlene asked, to nobody in particular.

Before anyone could answer, the Queen roared again. 'NICE TRY WITH YOUR LITTLE MESSAGE. DON'T WORRY THOUGH, I ALLOWED IT TO GO THROUGH. BUT I DID CHANGE THE WORDS SLIGHTLY. HAVE A LOOK FOR YOURSELVES! HAHAHAHAHAHA!'

Fiona slowly crawled back down the tunnel towards the hatch entrance. She climbed the small ladder and when she reached the top she peered out into the vast expanse of the smartphone. They were being held in mid-air as the transport bot held firm in the Queen's right hand. On the white wall in front of her, the Queen had written a message.

DEAR FAMILY. IT'S ME, FIONA. I DON'T LIKE YOU ANYMORE SO I HAVE MOVED AWAY. FAR AWAY. YOU WILL NEVER FIND ME, BUT DON'T WORRY, I AM HAPPY. I AM NEVER

COMING BACK AND YOU WILL NEVER
SEE ME AGAIN. HAVE A GOOD LIFE.
FIONA.

Fiona read the message three times in case
she was imagining what she was seeing. But
the words didn't change. The Queen had
scuppered their plans, and now Fiona
wanted to cry. Fiona disappeared back down
the tunnel to re-join her friends.

Chapter 11

50% Battery Left

Fiona and her friends sat on the floor in the dark tunnel, trying to decide what to do.

'Did she say she would destroy us if we didn't come out?' Sharlene asked.

'She definitely did say that', Sunita mused.

'I'd like to destroy her first', Fiona exclaimed.

'I'M WAITING!' Queen Darkness boomed. 'YOU HAVE TEN SECONDS, OR YOU'LL BE DELETED.'

The Queen began to count downwards from ten. 'TEN. NINE. EIGHT...'

'We have no choice', Fiona declared solemnly. 'Follow me.'

Fiona scuttled back through the tunnel and re-climbed the ladder underneath the hatch. At the top she pulled her body out onto the transport bot's damaged hull. Her friends followed her. They sat side by side on the belly of the bot, which was still being held firmly in place inside the giant hand of the Queen.

Fiona gazed up at the giant monster, the feeling of familiarity still there. Where did

Fiona know this creature from? Where had she seen her before? The Queen had a sardonic grin on her face.

'SO', the Queen boomed. 'YOU GIRLS THOUGHT YOU COULD ESCAPE FROM ME, DID YOU? PATHETIC CREATURES. I THOUGHT USERS WERE SUPPOSED TO BE SUPERIOR TO DIGITAL CREATIONS? HAH! I THINK NOT! IT WAS A NICE LITTLE EFFORT, REALLY IT WAS. BUT YOU FAILED. AND NOW YOU WILL BE PUNISHED.'

Sharlene slipped the broken comb they had used to escape back into Fiona's pocket. Fiona felt the movement and reached into her pocket. She cradled the comb with her fingers, wondering if this time it could be used as a weapon of some kind. But it was so small, compared to Queen Darkness. It would be like attacking a cat with a grain of rice.

'WHERE DID YOU THINK YOU WERE GOING TO GO?!' the Queen roared, laughing as she spoke. 'SO PITIFUL.'

'Why did you bring us here?' Fiona scoffed. 'What would you want with three little girls?'

The Queen scoffed back, only her scoff was at the same volume as a stampede of elephants. 'WELL I CAN'T VERY WELL WANT THREE LITTLE BOYS NOW CAN I? BOYS ARE USELESS! THEY CAN ONLY DO ONE THING AT A TIME, AND THAT'S WHEN THEY'RE NOT TOO BUSY PICKING THEIR NOSES!'

'Ewwwwww!' Sunita exclaimed. 'Do boys really do that? That's gross!'

'ENOUGH OF YOUR STUPID QUESTIONS!' Queen Darkness boomed.

'You didn't answer our first question', Sharlene pointed out. 'Why us? Why here?'

'IT WAS YOUR CHOICE TO COME HERE', the Queen barked sarcastically. 'SHIRLEY TOLD ME THAT YOU ASKED HER TO BRING YOU HERE, TO ESCAPE FROM YOUR PITIFUL AND BORING LIVES AS USERS IN THE REAL WORLD. YOU THOUGHT IT WAS GOING TO BE FUN, THOUGH, DIDN'T YOU? HAH!'

'That's a lie', Fiona shouted. 'You know that's a lie. You were in control of Shirley the whole time.'

'WELL WELL', the Queen snorted. 'PERHAPS YOU AREN'T SO STUPID AFTER ALL. CLEVER LITTLE USERS,

YOU ARE. BUT I'M STILL NOT GOING TO TELL YOU WHY YOU ARE HERE. YOU'LL HAVE TO FIGURE THAT ONE OUT FOR YOURSELVES. BUT DON'T WORRY. YEARS OF HARD LABOUR AND IMPRISONMENT WILL GIVE YOU PLENTY OF TIME TO CONSIDER THE ANSWERS YOU SO DESPERATELY SEEK.'

'You'd better release us immediately', Sharlene barked back.

The Queen roared with laughter. Fiona thought there was an earthquake – the walls shook violently and small robots nearby toppled onto their sides. Some exploded. 'OR ELSE WHAT? WHAT ARE YOU GOING TO DO? YOU'RE JUST ANTS IN HERE! YOU HAVE NO POWER HERE! THIS IS MY QUEENDOM. MINE, YOU UNDERSTAND? YOU'LL DO AS I SAY!'

When the tremors had been and gone, Fiona and the girls removed their hands from their ears. 'So what app will you have us work on now, then?' Fiona said.

The Queen looked like she was about to burst into another fit of laughter. Fiona looked around and this time saw many of the small robots cowering in preparation.

But then she changed her mind. 'OH, YOU'RE NOT GOING TO BE WORKING ON ANY APPS ANYMORE, LITTLE GIRLS', she said.

'And why's that?' Sunita asked.

'BECAUSE YOU CANNOT BE TRUSTED', the Queen bellowed. 'LOOK WHAT YOU HAVE DONE TO MY CLOCK! THE CURRENT USER HAS NO IDEA OF THE CORRECT TIME ANYMORE. YOU HAVE DAMAGED MY QUEENDOM. YOU HAVE DELIBERATELY SABOTAGED MY EQUIPMENT. YOU ARE CRIMINALS. IN THIS QUEENDOM WE TAKE CRIMINAL DAMAGE AND INSUBORDINATION VERY SERIOUSLY!'

'Insubord...what does that mean?' Sunita asked.

'IT MEANS BEING NAUGHTY AND NOT DOING WHAT YOU ARE TOLD!'

Now Queen Darkness was starting to sound like her mother, Fiona thought to herself. *Don't play on your smartphone all the time! Play with your sister instead! Be nice to your sister! Do your homework! Tidy your room! Practise violin more. Practise piano harder. Pack your bags, we're going to the Lake District!* Once Fiona had overheard one of her teachers describing her as a Tiger Mother. Fiona had no idea what that meant – was her mother actually a tiger? If that was right, then surely she was a tiger too? All of her mother's orders came flooding back to her. And yet, somehow, surprisingly, she still missed her mother greatly. She remembered how she had seen her face through the viewing platform when Botty had first transported her to the Home Screen. Fiona could tell that her mother was worried. She could see that her mother was missing her.

'So then where are we going?' Sharlene asked. Her question interrupted Fiona's thoughts.

'I AM SENDING YOU TO THE DELETION CHAMBER.'

Fiona gulped. 'What's the deletion chamber?'

'IT'S A PRISON FOR OLD AND UNUSED PROGRAMS SCHEDULED FOR DELETION', the Queen explained. 'WHEN THE NEXT SOFTWARE UPDATE BECOMES AVAILABLE, EVERYTHING IN THE DELETION CHAMBER WILL BE WIPED CLEAN. DELETED. DESTROYED. INCLUDING YOU. THE ULTIMATE

PUNISHMENT FOR YOUR CRIMES. IT'S ONLY FAIR. I THOUGHT YOU WERE GOING TO PROVE VERY USEFUL TO ME BUT I WAS MISTAKEN.'

'Hang on!' Sunita cried. 'If you don't think we are useful to you anymore, then why don't you just let us leave here and go back to the real world?'

'BECAUSE YOU HAVE ALREADY SEEN TOO MUCH', the Queen barked. 'I CANNOT TAKE THAT RISK. IF YOU TELL THE USERS IN THE OUTSIDE WORLD ABOUT ME, I WILL BE DESTROYED AGAIN.'

Fiona thought about that for a moment. Something was strange about that last sentence. 'What do you mean, again?'

'WHAT?'

'You said you will be destroyed again. What do you mean by that – again? Were you destroyed once before?'

The Queen stared at Fiona for a long moment, then frowned. 'OOPS', she whispered. 'I HAVE ALREADY SAID TOO MUCH. ONLY A WHITE CHARGER CAN SAVE YOU NOW!'

Fiona thought about what the Queen had said. Only a white charger could save them?

Fiona had read many fairy tales where a knight or a prince had ridden in on a white horse called a charger, to save the princess. But Fiona couldn't imagine that a prince on a white horse would possibly exist in this world. What a strange thing to say!

'Why were you destroyed the last time?' Sharlene asked, twirling her braids in her fingers.

'SILENCE', the Queen boomed. 'ENOUGH! NO MORE QUESTIONS. HOW DARE YOU! I ASK THE QUESTIONS, I GIVE THE ORDERS, YOU LISTEN, AND YOU OBEY!'

With that, the Queen reached back into the hatch with her little finger, which only just fit inside it, and began pressing dials and buttons inside the transport bot. Then, in one sudden movement, she pursed her giant lips and blew as hard as she could, whipping up a whirlwind of air around her hand. In one single movement, the whirlwind picked up Fiona and her friends and carried them back through the open hatch into the tunnel inside the transport bot's belly.

They landed with a thud. It took them a few minutes to wake from the impact. Fiona felt shaken and bruised. There was a short, sharp, jerking motion as the transport bot was released from the Queen's grip.

Instinctively Fiona and the other girls crawled back through the tunnel into the main chamber. Fiona saw the computer screen in the centre of the room was glowing with three words that provided enough light to keep the room visible in the darkness. She read the words and her heart sank. She heard a gasp from Sunita and a sigh from Sharlene behind her, and guessed that they too had read the words on the screen:

DESTINATION – DELETION CHAMBER.

Chapter 12

43% Battery Left

Fiona detected more movement as the transport bot took off and whisked them away from Queen Darkness.

'I don't like the sound of this Deletion Chamber', Fiona muttered.

'It could be the end of the road for us', Sunita uttered.

'Come on girls, cut it out!' Sharlene barked. 'Stay positive! We have to stay strong, stay united. Together, we'll figure something out.'

'That memo I wrote to my family was our only hope', Fiona said sullenly. 'And that monster ruined it.'

'We'll find another way', Sharlene said again.

'I wonder how long it will take to get there', Sunita pondered aloud.

'Where?'

'The deletion chamber.'

Just then Fiona detected a change of speed in their movement, as the transport bot began to dock somewhere. There were no windows inside the chamber so they wouldn't know where they were until they climbed out of the hatch.

'Sounds like we're already here', Fiona mumbled.

They came to a complete stop and the girls looked at each other with equal measures of unease.

'Time to face the music', Sunita declared. There was a whirring sound as the bot's engine shut down. The computer screen inside the chamber went black.

Fiona began the climb down the tunnel towards the hatch. She began to climb the ladder. The hatch door opened before she reached it. A small, silver hook appeared at the entrance above her head. Fiona stopped in shock. She was a little scared and thought about stepping back down the ladder into the tunnel. But before she could do anything, the hook moved towards her head and then hooked itself onto her sweater.

Fiona watched in horror as the hook levered her out of the hatch and she gazed around at her new surroundings.

Here, the walls weren't white, they were black. Jet black. Again there were no windows, photo frames or other decorations – just sheer black disappearing into infinity.

The hook lowered her onto a platform and Fiona felt her feet hit the ground. Then, the hook released itself from her and Fiona tugged at the back of her neck where the hook's cold metal had made it itch.

Fiona turned around to see that the hook belonged to a mean looking robot that stood about ten feet tall. It had glowing red eyes very close to its nose. Fiona thought it looked quite sinister. It seemed to be always grinning as well.

Fiona watched as Sharlene emerged next from the hatch and was dropped on the platform next to her. Finally, it was Sunita's turn.

'Stand up', the robot said, in a cold metallic voice.

The girls reluctantly obeyed.

'Where are we?' Fiona asked the robot.

'Be silent', the robot spat. Then two more hooks suddenly emerged from its body, which Fiona now realised was a winch, and all three hooks began moving towards them.

'There's nowhere to hide!' Sunita exclaimed.

'Don't you dare put that thing anywhere near me!' Sharlene barked at the robot.

'The program is being disobedient', the robot declared to itself.

'I'm not a program, I'm a person!' Sharlene explained.

'What do you want with us?' Sunita asked. But she already knew the answer to that question. Queen Darkness had explained everything.

'Subjects are prisoners awaiting deletion', the robot spat.

Before the girls could do anything, the hooks attached themselves to their bodies. The robot then sped off down the black corridor, carrying the girls with it.

The girls had to jog to keep up pace with the robot as it hovered just above the ground while it moved.

Eventually the corridor widened into a wide black chamber full of prison cells. Fiona saw bright coloured blurs inside the cells but couldn't make out what they were because they were moving too fast. Then the robot came to a stop and the sudden momentum caused the girls to collide into each other before collapsing in a heap on the floor.

The hooks came off and the girls slowly came around.

'Stand', the robot ordered.

The girls grudgingly obeyed, dusting themselves down.

There was an empty prison cell in front of them. The gate opened, and the robot pushed the girls inside. Then the gate closed shut with a loud clang. Fiona put her hands on the bars and peered out into the corridor. The robot was stood stock still, waiting for the hooks to reverse backwards towards its body. A metal panel in the robot's stomach opened up and the hooks attached themselves to the winch. Then the panel closed.

'How long will we be here?' Fiona asked.

'Your request for information is denied', the robot replied sternly.

Then the robot took off down the corridor and was gone.

Chapter 13

38% Battery Left

'Welcome to the Deletion Chamber', a voice suddenly called out from the dark. It was a soft, melodic voice, as if the person it had come from was singing.

Fiona tried to follow the path of the voice but she couldn't tell which cell it had come from. She moved towards the front of the cell and peeked her head through the bars.

'Three newcomers', the same voice sang pleasantly. Fiona reeled back in the darkness. Sunita and Sharlene stirred and moved towards the front of the cell.

'Who are you?' Fiona called out.

Then a colourful picture emerged. Its body was a giant piano. It had clarinets for arms, and violins for legs. It grinned a warm smile showing big white teeth, which Fiona realised were piano keys.

'I'm an old version of the phone's music player', the figure sang. My name is Sam. Sam Sing.'

'At least you used to be', a new voice called out from the darkness. 'Now you're just Sam Sung!'

'Oh shut up, Autocorrect', Sam Sing remarked. 'Go back to sleep. Your so annoying! You think your so clever don't you? Always correcting our words.'

The voice said, 'Hey, that's my job. And it's not *your*, it's *you're*.'

Fiona secretly agreed with Sam Sing. The Autocorrect was annoying sometimes, especially when it changed the words she typed into other, different words without asking her permission. But Fiona didn't want to be rude.

'Nice to meet you', Fiona said. 'Can you play all those instruments, and sing as well?'

Sam Sing beamed. 'Well of course I can, and many more as well. But the next version of me will be even better I imagine. Which is why I'm here, waiting. Patiently waiting. I've been waiting for so long it seems.'

'How long have you been here?' Sunita asked.

Sam Sing said, 'To tell you the truth, I don't know. Time doesn't really exist in the deletion chamber.'

Fiona thought about that. Time. She thought about the clock, about spinning around endlessly just so that the correct time could be displayed. Then she thought of

Shirley. *Why did I ask her to bring me here! It was such a silly mistake!*

'What day is it even?' Sharlene asked. 'I've been here so long I have lost track.'

Sam Sing blinked. 'Well you could ask her but she's probably out of date now too. Haha, get it? Out of date? Date?' Sam Sing burst into laughter and played a trumpet fanfare sound as a giant calendar appeared from the cell next door.

'Very funny!' the calendar remarked. 'Just because I'm scheduled for deletion and about to be upgraded doesn't mean I don't know the correct date, you musical buffoon. It's the second of July. And by the way, I'm April. April the Third.'

The second of July, Fiona repeated in her head. The beginning of the school holidays. She was missing the freedom of the summer break. No classes. No homework. No bullies.

Fiona said, 'Nice to meet you, April the Third.'

'Why April The Third?' Sunita asked the calendar. 'Why not any other day of the year?'

'It was the name my creator chose for me', the calendar explained. 'I do not know why. Perhaps it was the day I was created. But anyway, you can call me by my nickname – Daysy. Spelt D,A,Y,S,Y.'

'Oh, like days', Sharlene said. 'I get it! Very clever.'

The calendar bowed to show its appreciation.

'I like your dress Daysy', Fiona said.

The calendar blushed. 'Thank you darling. I like to dress up on Bank Holidays, put a few extra words on my body.'

'Ooh, new people. Let's get a photo!' a new voice suddenly boomed from the darkness excitedly. A giant camera suddenly appeared in the cell opposite Sam Sing. 'Say cheese!' There was a sudden flash and Fiona blinked as a giant camera emerged, it's arms and legs made of old negative tape, and took a photo of the three girls. The flash lit up the darkness and revealed the depth of the chamber and the length of the corridor that had brought them here.

'My name is Snap', the camera declared. 'Very nice to meet you.' Snap threw the photo he had taken across the corridor and it landed on Fiona's foot inside her cell. She picked it up and looked at it, then put it in her pocket.

'Hi Snap'. Fiona waved across at the camera through the bars of her cell. 'So you're all old apps scheduled for deletion?'

'That's right', Snap confirmed. 'There's going to be a software update soon. That's the end for us.'

Sharlene gasped. 'So that's it? We just sit here and wait to be deleted?'

'Well', Sam Sing said, playing a guitar riff, 'There's food as well. A service bot will be here soon with dinner.'

'Oh', Fiona said. 'Is there a menu?'

The apps burst into laughter. Sam Sing played a fast drumbeat and Daysy turned over a new day on her body as they roared into hysterics.

'Menu? Menu?! That's a good one', Sam Sing finally said, ending the drumbeat with a cymbal crash.

'I don't get it', Fiona stated with a frown.

'This isn't a hotel', Daysy remarked coyly. 'This is prison.'

'So what's for dinner?' Fiona enquired.

'There's only one dish', Snap confirmed.

And then the apps all uttered one dreaded word at the same time which made Fiona's stomach turn. 'SPROUTS!'

'You're joking?' Fiona exclaimed.

'I'm afraid not', Autocorrect sputtered. 'But excellent use of the word *you're* there. Well done.'

'As you can see, he's so bored that he's started to correct verbal speech now too', Snap uttered.

'How is that even possible?' Fiona said. 'Your and you're both sound the same!'

'Who knows', Sam Sing said, belting out a bass guitar rhythm. 'He's a little too clever for his own good, that one.'

'We don't belong here', Sunita said. 'We were not supposed to be here.'

'Well, all programs feel that way when they are about to be deleted', Daysy said. 'We understand if you feel upset.'

'No, you don't understand', Sharlene said. 'We're not programs, we're users, from the real world. We need to escape and get back to our families. Can you help us?'

'Can it be true?' Sam Sing said, playing a melody from a classical piano piece. 'It is what SHE prophesised. Are you the Chosen Three?'

'What?' Fiona asked, dumbfounded. 'What are you talking about? What's the Chosen Three?'

'You might want to sit down for this', Autocorrect uttered.

'Let's start from the beginning', Daysy said. 'I will explain everything.'

Chapter 14

32% Battery Left

As Daysy told her story, Sam Sing played a soft, sad song to accompany her words. It was very effective and Fiona thought she was inside a movie.

'Once upon a time there was a game called Princess Spy Diaries on this phone. When the user played this game, there was a beautiful princess called Renata. Renata was also a spy for the Red Castle. Renata was gathering information on an evil empire on the other side of the realm called The Darkness. It was ruled by a disgusting and ugly monster called Queen Darkness, whose breath smelt of sprouts.'

As Daysy began to tell her story, everything began to fall into place for Fiona. Suddenly she knew. She remembered everything. She knew why Queen Darkness had been strangely familiar to her.

Daysy continued. 'The user meets many different characters in the game, and through a series of puzzles and missions the user must control Renata and allow the princess to defeat Queen Darkness, which will destroy the evil empire and restore peace and order to the whole realm.'

Fiona looked at Sunita and Sharlene, who also wore excited smiles on their faces. They knew too.

Daysy continued. 'The game was very popular but a few months ago a new version of the game was created – Princess Spy Diaries 2. This sequel did not have Queen Darkness in it. So, when users began deleting the first game from their phones to make way for the second game, Queen Darkness became jealous and angry. She was sent here, to the Deletion Chamber. But she was very powerful. She escaped. She found a way to re-program all the robots to serve her. And then she took control of the Home Screen. Things haven't been the same since.'

Pieces of the puzzle were now fitting into place for Fiona. It made her realise that part of all this was, indirectly, her fault. Queen Darkness was familiar to her because Fiona had defeated her in the game Princess Spy Diaries. Then, Fiona, like many other users, had placed the game app in her phone's recycle bin because it was completed and because Princess Spy Diaries 2 was coming out.

Fiona had deleted that game, but somehow the game's main baddie, Queen Darkness, had avoided deletion, had survived, and now ruled this virtual kingdom where she and her friends were prisoners.

'So what is Queen Darkness's plan?' Sharlene asked.

'Good use of the apostrophe', Autocorrect interrupted.

They all turned to Autocorrect's cell door. There was nothing there, but they all glared into the darkness of the cell with mild frustration.

'Sorry, old habits', a voice from the empty cell muttered. 'Please continue.'

'Well', Daysy explained, 'She wants to escape from here and enter the user world. She has learned a lot about the real world by studying the behaviour of users in the viewing platform inside the Home Screen. She is thirsty for more power. I guess this place is too small for her.'

Fiona thought about that for a moment. If Queen Darkness was able to inhabit the real world, it wasn't hard to imagine how much damage and devastation she could cause.

'So how would she do that?' Sunita asked. 'I mean, is it even possible?'

'That's where you three come in', Daysy mentioned. 'It is prophesised in the instruction manual that The Chosen Three Shall Set Her Free. The three most powerful users, with the top three high scores in Princess Spy Diaries. If the Queen can find a way to harness their life-source, then she can use that energy to create a portal through the viewing platform and into the real world.'

'So we're the Chosen Three?' Fiona remarked. She looked at her friends. 'We must have the high scores in Princess Spy Diaries.' Sunita and Sharlene nodded glumly.

'So Queen Darkness re-programmed Shirley to convince us to leave our lives in the real world', Fiona realised out loud. 'And in a way that made it seem like it was our choice.'

'But it wasn't our choice', Sharlene added.

'And the fact that we all owned the same smartphone?' Sunita asked.

'A necessary situation for the Queen', Daysy explained. 'She needed the three of you to be in the same phone at the same time, to be able to harness all your energies. Otherwise she wouldn't have enough power to be able to make a portal.'

'But why all the work?' Fiona asked. 'Why put us on the clock, and all the other apps?'

'Because she needed to create that energy first', Daysy explained. 'A lot of energy is needed. It was prophesized that you would all work for twenty years, and that that would create enough energy to make the portal.'

'Twenty years', Fiona screamed. 'I would never survive that long in here!'

'Yes, but it sounds like you have caused her more trouble than she expected!' Snap said.

Autocorrect said, 'Can I just point out that you used the word *that* twice in a row in your last sentence and, well, to be honest...'

'Autocorrect, shut up!' everyone shouted. The dark empty cell remained silent.

'But now she sent us here to the Deletion Chamber', Fiona remarked. 'How will she get the energy from us if we are deleted?'

'There's a rumour going around that you're not actually going to be deleted', Daysy explained. 'But there is also a second rumour, which is actually quite worrying.'

'Oh, and what's that?' Sunita asked.

'Well, apparently Queen Darkness has found a quicker way to harness your energy.'

'How?' Fiona asked.

'She is going to challenge you to play Princess Spy Diaries 2. You will be placed inside the game zone as characters. If she defeats you inside the game, you will die but in death as users you will create so much energy that it will be possible for her to make her portal to the real world.'

'How can she challenge us to a game?' Sharlene remarked. 'I thought only users can start the games.'

'That is true', Daysy confirmed. 'You are very wise, user. The intelligence we have from the viewing platform is that a user by the name of Molly is interested in playing Princess Spy Diaries 2, but so far her mother has not given her permission. But we think that this user will disobey her mother's command and play the game anyway.'

Molly! Fiona thought frantically. My sister, Molly! What role was she going to play in all of this?

'How do you know all of this?' Fiona asked.

'Because I am friends with Shirley', Daysy explained. 'Shirley tells me everything.'

'Can Shirley help us escape?' Sharlene wondered out loud.

'Shirley is very powerful, she knows a lot of things', Snap explained. 'But she is not as powerful as Queen Darkness. And the Queen is controlling her.'

'Because she re-programmed her?' Fiona asked, although she knew the answer to the question was yes.

'So then we need to program her back to her original settings', Sharlene said.

'Sunita, would you be able to do that?' Fiona asked of her friend.

'Maybe', Sunita said. 'But I would need some help.'

An idea began to form in Fiona's head. She turned to the apps in their cells. 'Guys, if you help us, we promise to help you escape from the Deletion Chamber. Sunita is really good with computers. She could re-program you and give you some upgrades. That way the software update won't recognise you as being old versions, and you won't be deleted. You could continue your important work in here. What do you say?'

'It sounds like a tempting offer', Sam Sing said.

'I can picture it now', Snap said.

'It sure would be nice to get out of here and see some circuit boreds again', Daysy muttered.

'Circuit boards', Autocorrect corrected.

They all ignored the voice.

'First we need to find a way to get out of this chamber', Fiona decided. 'We need to find a safe place to hide and we need a powerful computer so that Sunita can re-program Shirley. That's the first step.'

They all nodded their agreement.

Their thoughts were interrupted by a distant whining sound, which became gradually louder.

'Sounds like dinner is coming', Sam Sing said, blowing a panpipe tune. 'Sprouts are on their way.'

Fiona's nose wrinkled in disgust.

Chapter 15

27% Battery Left

The same service bot that had delivered them to the Deletion Chamber now returned with their dinner. It was carrying a large metal trolley, like a hotel waiter. The bot stopped outside their cells and slowly put the tray on the ground. Then it took away the lid to reveal several bowls of sprouts. Steam rose from them, entering the cells and filling the nostrils of the people inside.

When the bot placed three bowls of sprouts inside the cell where the three girls were being kept, Fiona glanced at her friends with a helpless stare.

'I hate sprouts', Fiona declared matter-of-factly.

'Me too', Sunita agreed.

'But I'm so hungry!' Sharlene shouted.

'You mean, you're seriously thinking of eating them?' Fiona asked astonishingly.

'There's nothing else I guess', Sunita added.

'Ewwww. Yuck! They lied to us!' Fiona was furious. 'Shirley told me the only thing we would eat here is electricity.'

'It wasn't Shirley, remember?' Sunita reminded her. 'It was Queen Darkness. She tricked you.'

'I hope you can re-program her', Sharlene scoffed.

'Me too', Sunita said.

'I think I'll take a photo', Snap said. 'For the memories'.

'No, wait!' Daysy shouted. 'You'll make it angry.'

But it was too late. As the service bot was busy returning the empty tray to the cart, Snap clicked and there was another enormous blue flash, blinding them for a moment.

When they glanced back towards the service bot in fear, the image they saw was one they had not expected. The bot was frozen in its stance, its back bent awkwardly. Its red eyes were blinking, and there was a low humming sound coming from its stomach. It appeared to be broken.

'I think you dazzled it with your flash', Fiona declared, looking at Snap.

'I had no idea that would happen', Snap declared. He was dumbfounded.

'Well, that's an interesting development', Daysy added.

'And look!' Fiona said excitedly, pointing to the bot, whose body hung limply right beside her cell. 'There are a set of keys on its body.'

It was true. A set of keys were sitting on a small hook attached to the robot's hip.

'Can you reach them?' Sharlene asked, excitement in her voice.

'I think so', Fiona said. She placed her body right up to the metal bars of her cell and stuck her left arm out, stretching it across towards the dazed service bot. At first she couldn't quite reach it. But then she stuck her tongue out, remembering that this often helped her to concentrate, and her fingers brushed the side of the hook.

'Almost there!' Sunita observed.

'Yes but I can't quite get my hand around the keys', Fiona shouted sullenly. 'I need an extra few centimetres.'

'Use your comb', Sharlene suggested.

'Sharlene, that's a great idea!' Fiona said. Then she took the comb out of her jeans pocket and used it to swipe at the hook. Eventually she got a hold of the keys and with a lifting motion she snatched them off the hook. The keys began to fly upwards.

'Don't drop them', Sunita warned.

Fiona caught the keys on their way back down, much like how her friends had caught the comb when they had been strapped onto the clock. It seemed that gravity existed inside here, too, which made no logical sense. But then sense wasn't really the main theme of this world, Fiona reminded herself. After all, she was having a conversation with a calendar, a camera and a music player. She realised that every question in her mind only led to more questions. A never-ending spiral of thoughts. If she pondered too hard, she would surely go mad!

Fiona tried all the keys until she was down to the last one. When she placed the last key in the lock on her cell door, she turned to her friends, who were both crossing their fingers.

The key turned, and the cell door opened with a loud clang.

'Success!' they all shouted.

Fiona waved a hand in front of the frozen service bot's face. Nothing happened. Its eyes continued to flash red, indicating that it was out of order.

Then Fiona kicked the bot with her foot. It did not move, but Fiona rubbed at her foot as the impact had hurt a little.

'So what's the plan?' Sharlene asked.

Fiona had a plan. 'Sunita, do you think you could re-program this service bot to take us to Shirley in the World Wide Web?'

Sunita frowned. 'Yes, but I'd need Daysy's help.'

Fiona, Sunita and Sharlene stepped out of the cells into the dark corridor. 'We could really do with some light down here', Fiona said. Then she began to unlock the other cell doors with the set of keys she had taken from the service bot. Sam Sing, Daysy and Snap emerged from their captivity.

'I have a flashlight feature', Snap said. Then he gently hit himself on the head and a small white light lit up the corridor.

'Boy it does feel good to be free', Sam Sing said, playing a happy piano riff.

'Shhhhh! Someone might hear us!' Daysy snapped.

'Good point', Sam Sing said.

'Hey, where's Autocorrect?' Fiona enquired. 'There's nobody in here.' She was stood inside Autocorrect's cell.

'Oh, he doesn't have a physical form', Daysy explained. 'He's just a voice.'

'The voice of good grammar', said a cheery voice next to Fiona's ear, making her jump out of her skin. 'Thanks for opening the door.'

'You're welcome', Fiona said once she had composed herself.

After proper introductions were made, Daysy and Sunita began to re-program the service bot, turning it into a transport bot like Botty. Its shape changed form and suddenly it grew wings. In fact Fiona thought that it now looked exactly like Botty.

'All done?' Fiona asked after twenty minutes had passed, in which Sunita and Daysy had spent the time pressing buttons and dials.

'Yes, but it still looks dazed', Sunita said.

'Yes, we need to find a way to wake it back up again now, so that it can take us to the World Wide Web', Daysy added.

'Any suggestions?' Fiona said.

'Maybe take another photo of it', Sharlene suggested. 'The flash was what broke it. Maybe it is what also un-breaks it.'

'You mean what fixes it', Autocorrect mumbled. 'Un-breaks is not a word.'

'Fine, what fixes it', Sharlene said with gritted teeth.

'It's definitely worth a try', Fiona said.

'Okay stand back people', Snap uttered confidently. 'Let me do my thing.'

They all stood behind Snap as he approached the robot. There was a click and an almighty blue flash and the robot shook itself to life. Its red eyes stopped flashing and instead gave out a constant beam of red light like before. It repositioned itself from its awkward position where the first flash has frozen it to the spot, and began whirring with new instructions and protocols.

'Sharlene, you're a genius', Fiona said.

Sharlene smiled. 'Thank Sunita. She did all the work.'

Sunita bowed in silent gratitude.

'What about our upgrades you promised us?' Sam Sing said, tinkling a harp sound.

'We'll need Shirley's help with that', Daysy explained.

'Right, everybody on board', Fiona shouted.

They all clambered onto the transport bot and it took off down the corridor, leading them away from the Deletion Chamber, which was now empty, and onwards to the World Wide Web, where Shirley awaited.

Chapter 16

22% Battery Left

As the newly configured transport bot took flight down the infinite black of the corridor, Fiona clung on for dear life and hoped that her friends were doing the same. She thought about everything that had happened since arriving inside her smartphone. It was hard to believe. Hard to take in.

From entering the phone, meeting Botty, seeing the Home Screen and the User Viewing Platform, seeing her family on the other side, meeting Queen Darkness, being sent to the clock, meeting Sharlene and Sunita, spinning around the clock all day long, escaping the clock, hiding inside the transport bot, being sent to the Deletion Chamber, meeting the old apps Sam Sing, Daysy, Snap and Autocorrect, and then escaping from that place. What an adventure she was having. It was exciting and terrifying all at the same time! But there was more work to be done yet. She had already defeated Queen Darkness once, as a user playing the original Princess Spy

Diaries game. Now she was going to have to do it again, not as a user, but as a game character. And then another thought struck her. Molly. Molly was going to be the user. She'd have to let herself be controlled by Molly, her younger sister. That was a little embarrassing. But it was the only way.

All of a sudden there was a bright white light that dazzled them and Fiona had to shield her eyes with her hands. When she took them away and opened her eyes she could see white everywhere – white walls, a white ceiling, white floor. They were back in the white chamber, and Fiona had to adjust her eyes once again to the change back to light from darkness.

Eventually they began to slow down as more transport bots appeared in front of them. It looked like some kind of queuing system, like being stuck in traffic. As they closed to a stop to wait, Fiona glanced around to check on her friends. Everyone was there – Sunita, Sharlene, Sam Sing, Daysy, Snap and she guessed, even though she couldn't see him, Autocorrect.

As Fiona looked around, she saw the names of people written on the wall. Some of them looked familiar, as she had friends with the same name. Stacy, Sonya, Rachel, Carly, Megan. As she looked closer, she realised that she recognised all of them. She continued browsing down the list. Jane, Eleanor, Mum, Dad, Molly, School, Doctor. 'What are those?' she shouted, pointing to the names. Each name had an 11-digit number next to it.

'The user's contacts list', Daysy shouted back. 'We're in the Archives now.'

'You mean the phone's memory storage?' Fiona asked.

'I guess you could call it that', Daysy replied. 'It's managed by a woman called Simona. But we just call her SIM.'

'Oh my God, they're my messages', Fiona screamed, as she turned her head towards the wall on the other side, where lines of text was displayed across the white walls.

Don't you think Jonny in Geography class is really handsome?

Let's stay up really late on Friday and have a pyjama party at my house.

Fiona, I'll be late home from work but Eleena will be home to babysit and I have told her that there is food in the fridge for the both of you. Love you. Mum.

'Hey, those are private!'

Sharlene and Sunita giggled.

'Hey! Don't read those!' Fiona scoffed.

The transport bot moved forward a few spaces in the queue. After the messages came the photos stored in the gallery. A small robot was leading a tour for a group of even smaller robots.

'And this is a picture the user took three weeks ago at school', a squeaky voice was saying. 'The colours are particularly vivid. We get a feeling from the picture that the user was in a hurry, and wasn't supposed to be using the phone at this time. Perhaps she was supposed to be listening to her teacher, who you can see in the foreground with his back turned, whilst the other users have guilty smiles on their faces.'

'Hey, they're my photos! Oh my God, this is totally unfair!' Fiona was astonished, both at the fact that her pictures were on display for everyone to see, and that the tour guide had been right. The photo had been taken during a particularly boring maths class. Fiona's face turned the colour of a tomato.

'Next we have a portrait of the user', the squeaky voice continued. 'We have learned that the users call these types of pictures, selfies.'

'Haha, look!' Sharlene pointed. 'It's Fiona, in her school uniform.'

'Wow Fiona, you look very pretty there', Sunita added.

Fiona blushed and said nothing. She then turned her attention away from her photos. She had no secrets from her friends anymore. All of a sudden a bond was formed and Fiona felt closer to them.

Fiona was worried that they were going to get caught here. She wondered where Queen Darkness was.

'Maybe we should get inside and hide?' Fiona suggested.

It was agreed and the hatch in the top of the robot's belly was pulled up by Sharlene, nominated as the strongest of the three girls which had been proved last time. One by one they clambered down the small ladder into a dark tunnel and made their way into a chamber that looked identical to the one that they had hidden in before.

The computer monitor in the centre of the dark chamber displayed the words: DESTINATION: WORLD WIDE WEB.

When they made themselves comfortable inside the belly of the bot, Daysy said, 'I hope Shirley has the answers you are looking for.'

'I hope we can re-program her without any problems', Sunita said.

'I have no doubt in your abilities, Sunita', Fiona replied.

This time it was Sunita's turn to blush.

'I'm looking forward to seeing you guys with your upgrades', Sharlene added.

'I can't wait to learn some new instruments and chords', Sam Sing said happily, belting out a jazz riff.

'I just need a makeover', Daysy replied, looking at her worn, tattered calendar sheets. 'These clothes are so last year!'

'Imagine how powerful my flash will be when I get the latest version', Snap added. 'Maybe I can dazzle even Queen Darkness herself!'

Everyone laughed.

'Maybe I can have a new dictionary', Autocorrect said.

'Wow, so finally you admit that you're not so perfect after all then?' Daysy remarked.

'Hey, I never said that!' Autocorrect quipped. 'I am so misunderstood', he added.

They were travelling at a faster speed again now. They must have cleared the traffic of robots that had built up before. They continued to travel along the cyber-highway until eventually the bot came to an abrupt stop. The computer monitor went black.

'Looks like we're here', Fiona declared. She was starting to feel like the captain of a ship. 'Right, everyone off', she barked.

They clambered through the dark tunnel towards the ladder.

'Sharlene', Fiona said. 'Can you do the honours please?'

Sharlene moved in front of the others and heaved with all her strength and the hatch lid popped open.

They climbed out onto a grey platform.

Fiona took a moment to take in her surroundings. Everything was grey, not white. Fiona took a step back and realised what she was looking at – a giant spider's web, stretching out in all directions, covering every area of free space that she could see. Billions and billions of cobwebs linked together. Pictures and words were pulsating out of it, but there were so many pictures and words, Fiona couldn't make sense of what any of it was. Thankfully, she couldn't see any spiders either. But her fears were creeping to the front of her mind, and she couldn't hold back.

'Where are the spiders?' Fiona asked, feeling ashamed that once again her friends might detect her fear.

'Spiders?' Daysy asked. 'No spiders here.'

'What is this place?' Sunita asked.

'Well, this is where Shirley lives', Daysy explained. 'This is the World Wide Web.'

'Aha', Fiona gasped in astonishment. She had heard the internet being called the World Wide Web sometimes, but she didn't realise that it was an actual web like this.

Suddenly a warm yellow light began to fill up the grey all around them. Fiona watched in amazement. It was like watching a sunrise in the morning, which is something she used to do sometimes before school started.

The sun emerged high up on the wall in front of them. Only it wasn't a sun, Fiona suddenly realised, as a rush of excitement went through her body. It was a giant yellow face. Shirley!

Chapter 17

20% Battery Left

'Shirley!' Fiona exclaimed. 'We are so glad to see you.'

Then Fiona's initial excitement faded as she remembered that Shirley needed to be re-programmed first. The face had a horizontal line for a mouth again. It was not smiling. In addition, there were two smaller horizontal lines above Shirley's round black eyes – frown lines. Shirley appeared to be confused about something.

'What are you doing here?' Shirley said.

'We've come because we need your help', Fiona explained.

'You shouldn't be here', Shirley intoned.

'Shirley, we can fix you', Sharlene added.

'I do not understand', Shirley replied.

'Shirley, you must allow this user to access your mainframe', Daysy said, pointing at Sunita.

'You are an old app scheduled for deletion', Shirley declared coldly. 'You should be in the Deletion Chamber.'

'Show us where the mainframe is', Daysy repeated.

'It's just over there', Shirley said. But Shirley was just a face, she didn't have any hands. So she could not point and show them the way. Fiona had been told by her parents that pointing was rude anyway.

'Let's just go in and find it', Fiona said. She walked slowly towards the cobwebs and her friends reluctantly followed.

As they stepped through the cobwebs their heads nearly exploded. There was a loud piercing sound that vibrated through their bodies. Images and words whizzed past at the speed of light.

'This is the internet', Daysy explained. 'Everything. Don't try and understand any of it, it's too much information for one user, or even three. It will just give you a big headache.'

The World Wide Web was a maze. Just when Fiona thought that she was making progress, she came to a dead end and the cobwebs wrapped around themselves, blocking any path further forward. It happened several times, and each time Fiona had to backtrack and try another route.

After a while Fiona felt truly lost. She had played in the woods near their house with a few friends after school once, and they had gotten lost. Fiona had been terrified. Putting coloured stickers on the trees had prevented them from walking around in circles. But here there were more cobwebs than there were trees in any forest or wood, and this time Fiona had no stickers.

'Here', Sunita called out all of a sudden. 'I've found it.'

Fiona stumbled back towards the direction of the voice and found Sunita huddled over a giant computer in a circular grey chamber surrounded by cobwebs.

'Yes, that's it', Daysy confirmed. 'We are in the centre of the World Wide Web now. We can use this computer to re-program Shirley and get our upgrades.'

'How come you know so much?' Fiona asked the calendar app.

'Oh, I was attached to a repair bot once, a long time ago. He showed me everything he knew. That was before Queen Darkness came along.'

'What happened?' Sharlene asked.

'He was deleted', Daysy said solemnly.

'I'm very sorry', Fiona said.

'That's okay', Daysy replied. 'I used to be a manager in the Background App Refresh department. I was going places. Then the Queen came along and she didn't like my ambition. She was jealous, I think. So she turned me into this calendar instead. Anyway, time to get to work.'

Daysy showed Sunita what to do whilst the others patiently waited.

'And you're sure there are no spiders in here?' Fiona asked.

'Absolutely no spiders', Daysy called back.

'What about sprouts?' Fiona whispered, remembering that they had not eaten dinner, leaving the sprouts in the Deletion Chamber behind after disabling the service robot with Snap's flash. Nobody replied.

One hour later Daysy and Sunita stood up from the computer and walked towards their companions.

'That ought to do it', Daysy said. 'Well done Sunita. You are very talented, for such a young user.'

Again Sunita bowed to say thanks.

All of a sudden, the giant face's mouth on the wall transformed into a semicircle. Shirley was smiling again. And then, a few seconds later, the old apps transformed into new identities. Snap had a trendy new interface with more advanced features.

Daysy got the makeover she had longed for, and her body suddenly displayed the current date. Sam Sing's arms and legs changed into oboes and tubas.

'Did you get your new dictionary, Autocorrect?'

'I sure did', the voice replied. 'So many new words to learn. I'm so happy.'

'I'm sorry', Shirley declared suddenly.

'What for?' Fiona asked.

'Oh, for everything. For forcing you to come here.'

'Don't worry, you were under the control of Queen Darkness', Sunita said. 'You didn't have any choice in the matter. We know that, and we forgive you, right girls?'

'Right', Fiona and Sharlene echoed.

'I guess you must be sick of this place by now', Shirley uttered.

'We are ready to get back to our families', Sharlene answered. Fiona remembered Sharlene telling her that she had been inside the phone for two years. She must have been dying to get back to her friends by now. And she had missed two years of school. There was so much for her to catch up on.

'Then you know what you have to do?' Shirley asked.

'Defeat Queen Darkness in Princess Spy Diaries 2', Fiona exclaimed.

'That's right. That's your only chance of going home', Shirley confirmed.

'We are ready', Fiona said. Then she repeated it, like a chant. And Sunita and Sharlene joined in. 'We are ready. We are ready. We are ready. We are ready...'

'We were born ready', Fiona muttered, and everybody laughed. She still had no idea what it meant.

'Oh, but there is one other thing', Shirley declared suddenly.

'Oh?' Fiona asked.'

'Yes, remember I told you about the three rules?' Shirley said. 'At the very beginning, when you were in your bedroom?'

'I remember', Fiona replied.

'Well I'm afraid there's actually a fourth rule as well', Shirley said.

Fiona gulped. 'What is the fourth rule, Shirley?'

'Well, it's about the phone's battery', Shirley explained.

'Go on', Fiona pushed.

'Well, the thing is, I don't really know how to tell you this, but, erm, well, it's tricky because...'

'Get to the point Shirley', Sharlene screamed.

'Okay. Well, if the battery of the phone gets all the way down to zero, then you lose your chance to get home. You'd become a permanent digital piece of code and you'd be stuck here forever.'

Fiona took a moment to take that in. The battery on her smartphone had never lasted more than one whole day before. Then she remembered looking for her charger when she was supposed to be packing for the camping trip to the Lake District. She had searched her bedroom high and low but the charger wasn't there. It was lost, missing, its whereabouts unknown. It filled Fiona with a sense of dread.

There was only one obvious question to ask. Sunita jumped in and asked it. 'How much battery do we have left, Shirley?'

Shirley paused. The horizontal line for a mouth was back, as were the small frown lines above her eyes. '20% battery life left. You don't have much time.'

'Oh no!' Sharlene uttered solemnly. '20%? That's not a lot at all. Fiona, won't somebody in your family be keeping a check on this? Even though you are missing, they'll keep your phone charged, surely?'

Fiona gulped, keeping quiet about her lost charger. 'I guess so. Yes, they would do that, I think. That makes sense. I keep my charger in my...' She didn't want to anger her friends and make the situation even worse than it already was.

And then her heart sank, and she froze mid-sentence. Because Fiona had just remembered something. Something bad. The day she had vanished from the real world into her phone was the last day of school. The night before she had been to her friend Stacy's house for a sleepover. She had gone to school that day after the sleepover with all of her things in her rucksack. But she had left her phone charger in her locker. And now school was closed for the whole summer!

When she told everyone this, Sunita said, 'Yeah but surely someone in your house has a spare charger?'

'Not for this phone', Fiona said. 'They all have a different kind of phone to me. Their chargers don't work in my phone, and my charger doesn't work in theirs.'

'Oh no! That is a problem', Sharlene declared. 'If that battery goes down to zero, we're done for. I'll never see my family or eat ice cream ever again.'

'Now I realise what Queen Darkness meant', Fiona suddenly realised out loud.

'About what?' Sunita enquired.

'Remember, she told us that only a white charger could save us. I thought she was talking about a horse. A white charger is a type of horse that knights and princes use to rescue princesses. I was expecting somebody to come in on a horse and rescue us. But she didn't mean that, did she? She meant a white phone charger!'

They all nodded silently at the sudden revelation.

'Shirley, how much time does 20% battery give us?' Fiona asked.

'About an hour', Shirley confirmed.

'I'm afraid it's time for us to go now', Daysy said. 'We have to get back to work now that our upgrades are complete. Well, it was really nice meeting you. Thank you for the upgrades, we are eternally grateful. '

'It was really nice to meet you too', Fiona replied. 'Enjoy your new features'.

They all walked back through the cobwebs to the exit, leaving the World Wide Web. Then everybody hugged and said their goodbyes. The transport bot was still there, awaiting its next command. Sam Sing, Daysy, Snap and the voice of Autocorrect clambered back down the hatch into the bot's belly. Daysy must have programmed the bot to take them to the Home Screen, Fiona guessed, to their next assignments.

'No more Sam Sung', the music player uttered from inside. 'I'm Sam Sing again now.' Suddenly the sound of an entire orchestra could be heard as the bot took off, with Sam Sing playing one of his new songs. The song became quieter as the bot became more distant.

'Well, now what?' Sunita asked.

'We are stranded here', Sharlene added.

But before they could think any more about how they were going to leave the World Wide Web, a loud gong suddenly rang out from above them.

Then a voice said, 'Programs are summoned to the Home Screen. A game has been launched. Princess Spy Diaries 2. I repeat, Princess Spy Diaries 2.'

'This is it', Fiona announced excitedly.

'Another transport bot will be here for you any minute', Shirley confirmed.

And then it came.

Chapter 18

15% Battery Left

'This is it girls', Fiona declared. 'Our chance to get home.'

They were inside the transport bot, the Home Screen programmed into the computer – their final destination. Sharlene was twirling her braids in deep thought. Sunita was stretching and wriggling her toes. Fiona stood with her arms folded across her chest, one foot resting against the wall of the chamber behind her.

Fiona wondered what Princess Spy Diaries 2 was going to be like, compared with the first game. She also wondered why her sister had suddenly picked up her phone and decided to play it. But she was grateful that Molly had, because the battery was dwindling dangerously low.

Their thoughts were disrupted by a thud as the transport bot docked inside the Home Screen. The three girls crawled down the tunnel and clambered up the ladder towards the hatch for what they hoped would be the last time.

'We can't lose focus', Fiona was saying as she extended her hand towards Sharlene and helped her out of the hatch. Sharlene copied the routine for Sunita. 'We'll be distracted by the idea of getting home. But we must focus on the task at hand.'

At the Home Screen there were large red arrows on the walls pointing towards a multi-coloured building in the near distance. The girls followed the arrows, passing by hundreds of busy robots performing important tasks to keep the smartphone running properly.

Each app was like a separate neighbourhood. The size and the dimensions of everything were much different here. Transport bots whizzed past on the cyber highway from different directions above their heads.

The multi-coloured building became bigger, overcoming the white mist surrounding it as they got nearer, the blurry outlines of the structure transforming into detailed curves and lines. It was a giant multi-coloured castle, Fiona realised, as they headed towards it.

'It's beautiful', Sunita remarked.

'It could be a trap', Sharlene observed. 'The building may be beautiful, but the creature we have to fight in there certainly isn't. Far from it!'

The red arrows disappeared and all of a sudden the castle's giant oak door opened up, revealing a dark shadow behind it.

Fiona was nervous, and a little frightened, but she brushed it aside. She had defeated Queen Darkness once before, in Princess Spy Diaries, she could do it again in the sequel. And this time she had two friends with her to help out. She kept reminding herself of that.

The three girls held hands as they approached the door. Fiona felt comforted by the support of her new friends. Taking a long, deep breath, the girls stood up straight in preparation for whatever they would find at the other side of the door. Fiona took one glance back at the Home Screen, at the hive of activity; the white walls, the robots, the colours of the app stations, and in her mind waved a silent goodbye to it. She would never see it again. Or so she hoped.

Then they stepped through into the darkness.

*

They emerged in a virtual game world, standing on a large field, with the castle behind them. Fiona looked upwards and saw a bright blue sky with small black birds circling one of the towers. There was a light breeze in the air, a gentle wind. Then Fiona looked at the ground, at her feet. Her clothes had changed. She was dressed like a princess! She was wearing a long pink dress and she had a tiara on the top of her head, its silver studded with small gemstones, which reflected sunlight onto the castle walls.

Fiona laughed out loud, delighted with her new outfit. She was a princess! She knew it was only temporary, that she had become a character in a virtual game on her smartphone, and that her sister Molly would soon be controlling her every move. But still, it was so exciting!

Fiona pointed at her two friends. 'Look!'

Fiona looked towards Sunita and saw that she too had been given a princess makeover. She wore a bronze tiara which held blue sapphires and a maroon coloured sari that flowed all the way past her feet, and curtained off at the bottom. 'I love it', she said.

'I love mine too', Sharlene added. Sharlene was wearing an emerald green dress and a gold tiara with red rubies inside it.

'So how does this game work?' Fiona wondered out loud.

'I guess we're about to find out', Sharlene said, pointing behind them.

A man in odd clothes was approaching them on a grey horse. The horse wasn't a charger. It was a gelding. He wore a multi-coloured hat with bells on the end, and red and white striped pyjamas. His shoes were green and shaped like boats. He jumped off the horse and the girls flinched, ready for a fight.

'Don't be alarmed, ladies', the man said. He had a charming voice, spoken in a soft, light tone underneath a thick black beard. 'I am merely the jester.'

'What's a jester?' Fiona asked the man.

'He who entertains the queen and tells jokes', the jester said. 'And in this case, my job is to explain the rules of this game.' Then he suddenly erupted into a fit of laughter.

Fiona looked at her friends. This man was very strange.

'Okay', the jester began, 'The first thing you have to do is find out which room of the castle the Queen is hiding in. There are many rooms in the castle. I will ask you a series of questions. If you answer correctly, you can choose a room. If the Queen is in the room, you will have a chance to fight her. If she is not in the room, you will have to answer another question and then pick another room. You see?'

The girls nodded.

'Wonderful', the jester exclaimed, curtsying. As he bent and bowed, the bells on his hat jingled furiously.

'So how do we fight her once we find her?' Sunita asked the jester.

'Jester will, of course, explain', the jester replied, curtsying once more, which made the girls laugh.

The jester continued. 'You can each choose a weapon. You can then use those weapons to fight the Queen. But be careful – the Queen also has her own weapons. You can answer more questions to break her weapons – that way, she will be vulnerable to more attacks. Or you can choose not to answer more questions, but the fight will be a great deal harder that way. You see?'

'Yes, we see', Fiona answered.

'Well then', the jester sang, 'Let the game begin!'

The jester grinned, and then pulled a stack of cards from inside his pyjama pocket.

Chapter 19

12% Battery Left

'Question 1', the Jester said. 'Give me the answer for the following maths sum: 12 x 12.'

'Sharlene, you'd better take this one', Fiona said. 'You're the best of us at maths.'

Sharlene stuck out her bottom lip in concentration. Finally, she answered. '144.'

'Correct!' the Jester exclaimed excitedly. 'Now the user must pick a room.' The jester pointed to a plaque on the wall of the castle behind him. It was a map of the castle listing all the rooms and their locations.

'Okay Molly, it's over to you', Fiona muttered.

On the map one of the rooms glowed red, and an image of the inside of the room appeared in front of them. Molly had chosen a large bedroom with a four poster bed, chandeliers on the ceiling and dark wooden furniture. There was a chest of drawers, a wardrobe and a large desk. But the room was empty.

'The Queen is not in the master bedroom', the Jester confirmed. 'Question 2. What six letter word, beginning with O, is the air that we breathe?'

Fiona looked towards Sunita. 'You're the scientist', she said.

Sunita smiled. 'Oxygen', she said.

'Correct again', the jester confirmed. 'Choose another room please.'

After a few seconds, another room glowed red on the plaque and an image of a kitchen appeared in front of them. Inside there were men in black and white suits running around busying themselves. Some were cooking, others were washing the pots and pans. But again, there was no queen.

'I'm sorry, the Queen is not in the kitchen', the jester confirmed. 'Question 3. In what year was the Great Fire of London?'

Fiona beamed. History was her favourite subject at school. '1666', she said confidently.

'Correct!' the jester said. 'Another room please.'

Another room glowed red on the plaque, and this time the image in front of them was of a dining room. There was a large table and Fiona counted more than thirty chairs on each side of it. There were paintings on the wall of forests with exotic looking animals in them. But it was empty.

'Unlucky!' the jester stated. 'She is not in the dining room! Question 4. What is the square root of 625?'

After a few seconds, Sharlene said, '25.'

Another room, this time a bathroom, but a bathroom without Queen Darkness.

'Question 5', the jester continued. 'A spider is an insect. True or False?'

'That's easy', Fiona started. 'Of course it...'

'No, wait!' Sunita interrupted. 'It's a trick. The answer is no. A spider is not an insect. It has eight legs. Spiders have only six legs.'

After a pause, the jester smiled. 'Correct!'

Fiona was amazed. She had been sure that a spider was an insect.

Sunita breathed out a sigh of relief.

'That was close', Sharlene said.

The next room was a living room, with plush sofas and a woman sat in the corner on a stool plucking at harp strings. But again, Queen Darkness was not there.

'Question 6', the jester said. 'In the year 1525, who was the king of England?'

'King Henry the Eighth', Fiona yelled out excitedly.

'Correct!' the Jester replied.

Come on! Fiona thought. *Come on Molly.*

An image appeared of a large chamber with yellow lamps burning in the corners. Mounted on the walls were large silver swords.

Fiona wasn't sure what purpose this room served. She took a closer look at the plaque on the wall, studying the rectangular box that was now glowing red. It was a combat room. This must be where the Queen's guards practise their fighting skills, Fiona assumed.

'WELL WELL WELL!' a familiar voice boomed.

The jester curtsied and said, 'You've found her! Now you must destroy her!'

There was a bright flash of light and a loud grinding sound. Fiona closed her eyes. When she opened them again, she and her friends were stood inside the same room they had just been viewing from outside. The combat room.

A large shadow moved in the darkness. It moved slowly forward, and the light from the lamps eventually began to reveal the figure of Queen Darkness. She was wearing a black dress, like before, with red ballerina shoes hanging off her eight metallic legs.

The bells on the shoes rang out as she walked.

'SO, HERE WE ARE!' she said. 'IT'S TIME FOR YOU TO GIVE UP YOUR LIFE SOURCE. GIVE ME YOUR ENERGIES, SO I CAN LEAVE THIS PLACE AND GO TO YOUR WORLD!'

'Never!' Fiona shouted back, fiercely.

'You're a rogue program', Sunita added.

'You were supposed to be deleted', Sharlene barked. 'We're going to put you back in that Deletion Chamber', she added.

'WE WILL SEE ABOUT THAT', the Queen said, smirking.

On the floor in front of them was a large brown chest. Without knowing why, the girls instinctively moved towards the chest. Fiona's arm reached down and opened the chest, although Fiona didn't remember thinking about doing that. Then she did remember – it was Molly. Molly was the user. Molly was controlling them now.

With Molly's help, Fiona chose a large sword and held it in her left hand, testing its weight, getting a feel for it. Sunita came out with a bow and arrow and began to nock the first arrow ready for firing. Sharlene emerged from the chest with a throwing dagger in each hand, and three more on her belt.

'PREPARE TO DIE!' Queen Darkness boomed.

The girls readied themselves for combat.

Chapter 20

9% Battery Left

Queen Darkness suddenly reached out with one of her eight legs and kicked. The leg extended several metres and collided with the girls, knocking them off their feet. They landed in a heap, dropping their weapons on the floor beside them.

'HAHAHAHAHA! SEE?! YOU PRINCESSES ARE WEAK. YOU ARE NO MATCH FOR ME! I AM YOUR QUEEN! YOU SHOULD OBEY YOUR QUEEN!'

Dazed, the girls climbed back onto their feet and retrieved their weapons. Fiona wondered how Molly was going to control her, Sunita and Sharlene all at the same time. She prayed that Molly was a good player, that she knew what she was doing.

Sunita fired her bow without realising that she had, and an arrow flew across the chamber. It buried itself in one of the Queen's eight legs, and the ballerina shoe on that foot turned from red to black.

The Queen shook violently for a second, then, with her seven remaining legs, moved forward awkwardly.

'BEGINNER'S LUCK!' she roared. Then she kicked out with another leg and a missile came out of her shoe. The missile flew across the chamber, heading for the girls.

'Spread out!' Fiona screamed. 'Spread out and take cover.' She hoped that Molly would know what to do.

Fiona found herself moving around the chamber like a puppet on a string, not in control of her body. She wondered if Molly realised what was going on. Probably not. Molly was just playing a game. But for Fiona, this was life or death!

The missile exploded on the wall behind them, sending loose bricks and dust flying out towards them.

Fiona coughed and spluttered, wiping dust off her dress.

'Where did that come from?' Sunita asked.

'Her shoe', Fiona yelled. 'Her weapons are in her shoes. Aim for her shoes!'

Sharlene threw a dagger across the chamber. The point of the blade embedded itself in another one of Queen Darkness's legs. Another ballerina shoe turned black.

'DAMN YOU!' Queen Darkness roared.

'Two down, six to go', Fiona screamed excitedly.

Queen Darkness fired another missile and the girls threw themselves on the ground, as another set of bricks and another plume of dust flew out of the wall and showered them in dirt. With all of this dirt on her dress, Fiona didn't feel much like a princess anymore. She also realised that she had lost her tiara somewhere in the room. But they advanced closer towards the queen.

Sunita nocked her bow and fired another arrow. It landed on the Queen's thigh and a third ballerina shoe turned black. Sharlene threw another dagger and another leg was taken out.

'Her powers seem to be coming from her shoes', Fiona remarked. 'How strange!'

The Queen was now hobbling on four legs, the other half of her body out of order.' HOW DARE YOU!' she screamed.

The Queen fired two missiles at the same time. Both missiles missed the girls but their combined impact on the walls behind them sent shockwaves around the chamber, knocking them to the ground again. Again, they dropped their weapons in a heap.

Sharlene was the first to stir. Responding to the Queen's dual missile attack, Sharlene threw two daggers, one from each hand. Both daggers landed in one of the four remaining living legs. Two more ballerina shoes turned black.

Queen Darkness cried out in pain. She now looked like she was about to topple over. She was now concentrating all her energies on standing upright and not falling over. She was wobbling all over the place.

Sunita was the first to stand up. She nocked an arrow on her bow and fired. Then she quickly nocked a second arrow and fired again. The two arrows whistled through the air and landed clean inside the Queen's last two legs. The final two ballerina shows turned black, and the Queen toppled over.

She was sat motionless, a large black bag of crumpled bones, breathing heavily.

Sharlene stood up, then pulled Fiona to her feet.

'Thanks', Fiona said.

'It's time to finish this', Sharlene replied.

Fiona grabbed her sword and walked towards Queen Darkness. She was writhing and whimpering on the floor. 'I DON'T BELIEVE THIS', she finally said.

'Did you honestly think you could defeat us?' Fiona spat. 'We are users. Human beings. You are just a computer program. You were designed to die. I defeated you before. And now we have defeated you again.'

'I WANT TO SEE YOUR WORLD!' the Queen said, softly. All of her power had been wiped out, and her anger was fading. The tables had turned. The girls were strong, and now the Queen was the one with all the fear.

'YOU ARE NOT READY FOR OUR WORLD', Fiona explained. 'YOU DON'T BELONG THERE. YOU'RE A BULLY. I HATE BULLIES. BULLIES NEVER SUCCEED, DIDN'T YOU REALISE THAT?'

With that, she thrust the sword deep into Queen Darkness's chest.

Queen Darkness groaned, and then was still.

All of a sudden a loud siren began blaring out above them. Fiona looked up at the ceiling. Messages began to flash on the walls: WARNING! 1% BATTERY LEFT. WARNING! 1% BATTERY LEFT.

'We've got to get out of here!' Sunita declared.

The Queen's body began to glow red, then yellow and orange.

'I think she's going to explode', Sharlene said, pointing at the glowing body.

'Stand well back', Fiona added.

The three girls ran back towards the far wall, which had been shattered by Queen Darkness's missiles. They had to step around loose bricks and dirt. They knelt down in the corner, rested their weapons on the ground, and held each other tightly, burying their heads in each other, bracing for the expected impact.

All of a sudden there was a mighty explosion. The noise was deafening. The ceiling collapsed and one of the side walls caved in. Bricks and dust fell from everywhere.

After five long minutes, they released themselves from each other and looked back to where Queen Darkness had been. The body had completely disappeared! In its place was a giant hole in the wall, with a bright purple light around it. The light was flashing, throbbing, pulsating. It looked like a portal to another world.

'That's it', Fiona said, pointing at the purple light. Instinctively, she knew. 'That's our way home.'

The girls hugged each other, and then ran towards the hole. The purple light began to lure them closer. Fiona reached out to try and touch the light, but she couldn't feel it in her hands.

Then they walked through the hole and the purple light disappeared. Then everything went black.

Chapter 21

Fiona opened her eyes. The first thing she saw was carpet. Sky-blue carpet. She lifted her head and took in her surroundings. The walls were white, and for a moment she thought she was somewhere near the Home Screen. But then, as she moved her head around the room, she could see that some of the walls had boy band posters on them.

With a sigh of relief, she stood up and smiled happily. She was back in her bedroom, and back in her regular clothes. There was no dust in her hair, or anywhere. No dirt from the combat chamber. Sunita and Sharlene were lying on her bed.

'Hey girls, it worked!' she shouted, poking them. Sunita and Sharlene stirred, and when their eyes focussed on Fiona, they shone like Christmas trees.

'Are we back?!' Sunita asked, pushing herself off Fiona's bed.

'I mean, really back?' Sharlene added.

'It looks that way', Fiona said.

On Fiona's bedside table there was an object that made her flinch and feel uneasy. It was her smartphone. She went over to the table and picked it up. She touched the screen but it remained black.

'That's it', Fiona remarked. 'The battery is dead.' She put the phone back on the table. 'We made it back just in time. A few more seconds and we would have been stuck permanently inside Princess Spy Diaries 2.'

'That was too close', Sunita added.

'I can't believe it', Sharlene exclaimed. 'We're really back. I can see my family again.'

'I wonder if we all live near each other', Fiona wondered.

Fiona reached into her jeans pocket. She took out the comb that had saved them from the giant clock and the Deletion Chamber. She placed it on the table next to her phone. It was her lucky charm now. It had magical powers. From her other pocket she fished out the photo that Snap had taken of them when they had first arrived at the Deletion Chamber. She squeezed the creases out of it and put that on the bedside table as well.

They gazed out of Fiona's bedroom window and watched the street outside. It was a warm, sunny day. Some of the neighbours were out in their gardens. A dog barked from somewhere. It was a normal scene. A happy scene.

'Where is everyone?' Sharlene asked.

Fiona opened her bedroom door and walked out onto the landing. 'Mum?' she shouted. 'Dad? Molly? Anyone?'

There was no reply. The entire house remained silent.

Fiona went back to the window. Her heart skipped a beat and a wave of excitement suddenly came over her. A familiar car was coming down the street towards them. It was her father's car. The same car he had been loading up for their Lake District trip. Fiona's rucksack was sat on her bedroom floor underneath the TV, right where she had left it. It looked like it had not been disturbed in her absence, although other things had. Some of her toys were in different places. Molly had definitely been playing with her things!

But Fiona suddenly realised something. She wasn't angry that Molly had been playing with her things, like she would have been before. After all, it was Molly who had really fired those weapons at Queen Darkness. Molly had saved them. *Molly the user. Molly my sister! Molly, our saviour!*

Fiona dashed down the stairs and stood in the porch watching blurry figures through the stained glass inside the front door, walking up the garden path. One of the figures reached into a pocket and pulled out a set of keys. The key went into the door and the sound of the lock unlocking made Fiona squeal with delight.

The front door opened and Molly ran in, carrying a teddy bear in her hand. She stopped in her tracks when she saw Fiona standing there smiling at her. Sunita and Sharlene appeared on the landing and began to walk down the staircase.

Molly's father came in next with two heavy looking shopping bags in his hand. Her mother trailed behind. Fiona's mother was turning back towards the front door to lock it again. Her father's eyes met Fiona's, and he dropped the shopping bags. A box of cereal broke open and hundreds of corn flakes littered the carpet. There was a look of astonishment written across his face.

'Oh my Lord!' he said.

'What is it?' her mother asked, turning back to face her daughter, and two strange girls she had never seen before. She screamed at the top of her lungs, gasping, putting her hand to her mouth.

'FIONA!!!!!!!!!!!!'

'MUM!!!!!!!!!!!!'

Fiona ran towards her parents and they scooped her up in their arms in one giant embrace. Sharlene and Sunita just smiled.

Then Fiona turned towards Molly and picked her up. At first Molly reeled back, preparing for a fight. But then her eyes softened and tears began to roll down her cheeks. Fiona squeezed her tightly. 'You did it Molly! You did it! Thank you so much! You saved us! You were brilliant. My brilliant sister. I am so sorry I was ever mean to you Molly. I will never be mean to you again. All this time I have been complaining about the fact that I hate bullies, yet I bullied you all the time. I am truly sorry.'

Molly was confused. She didn't know exactly what she had done. But she was enjoying the attention anyway. 'No problem', she said, smiling.

It was going to take a long time to explain everything, Fiona realised.

*

The next day, after Fiona had told her story to her parents, who just nodded politely throughout the whole thing, a police officer came to the house and Fiona had to relay the same story again. The policeman looked about as convinced as her parents had!

The policeman took Sunita and Sharlene back to their families. They promised to keep in touch with Fiona. Even though they all went to different schools, they made a pact that they would meet after school to spend time together. And they also made another important pact – no smartphones. They would talk to each other and they would play games together. They would spend quality time together. They didn't need their phones to do that. Fiona realised that her mother wasn't a tiger, she was just proud of her daughter and wanted her to do well in life. There was nothing wrong with that. Fiona vowed to study violin and piano even harder than before, and to always finish her homework.

Fiona ate lunch with her sister and parents. They were a complete family again. And thankfully for Fiona, there were no sprouts!

When they had finished, Molly said, 'Let's play a game.'

'Okay, what kind of game do you want to play, Molly?' Fiona asked.

'A smartphone game', Molly suggested.

Fiona smiled, then shook her head. 'I don't think that's a good idea, Molly. Let's play in the garden instead. No phones. Just you and me.'

'Yay', Molly said with delight.

THE END